The Wicked

Thea Harrison

The Wicked

ISBN 10: 0989972828
ISBN 13: 978-0-9899728-2-6

Print Edition 1.0

Original publication in ebook format by Samhain Publishing:
The Wicked, 2013

This book is a work of fiction. The names, characters, places, and incidents are products of the writer's imagination or have been used fictitiously and are not to be construed as real. Any resemblance to persons, living or dead, actual events, locale or organizations is entirely coincidental.

Dedication

To the wonderful women who helped me by beta reading this story: Kristin, Anne, Andrea, Rene and Holly. And to Heather and Amy.

Chapter One

"You need me to stay home from school today, you know," Chloe mumbled around her last mouthful of homemade blueberry muffin before giving Olivia a sly, sidelong smile. Olivia smiled back at the little girl. Chloe was a tempestuous, high maintenance child, and Olivia adored her.

Olivia might be childless, but not because she didn't like children. She loved them. Besides, even if she hadn't liked children, she would have found it hard to resist Chloe's wily charm.

After Olivia and Chloe shared a smile, they turned to regard one of the most Powerful Djinn in the world. Khalil lounged at the head of the breakfast table like a Pasha reigning over a court of nobles.

Early morning sunlight slanted in the French doors behind him, glinting bright silver sparks off the ocean just on the other side of a wide, sandy beach. The sunlight touched Khalil's raven-black hair with a knifelike edge of white that gleamed as brightly as his strange, diamond-like eyes.

As the five-year-old squirmed impatiently in her chair, Khalil regarded her, genuine curiosity on his pale, regal features. "Please, do explain. Why do we need for you to stay home from school this time?"

Chloe opened her eyes wide. "Well, obviously, because Olivia has to leave today. It's the *very last day* of her week. You need someone to play with Max, so you can visit with her while you can." Her expression turned calculating. "I'd be doing you a favor, you know."

After having spent a week's vacation witnessing her friend Grace's eccentric lifestyle, Olivia had grown quite educated in the dynamics of the household. She sensed a tactical error in Chloe's last statement, and her gaze swiveled back to the Djinn expectantly.

Khalil raised a sleek back eyebrow at Chloe. "I believe it would be most unwise to become indebted to you. You have picked up the Djinn's love for bargaining all too well. Grace and I will somehow contrive to manage both Max and a final visit with Olivia. You will go to school as planned."

Storm clouds gathered in sky-blue eyes. "Max doesn't have to go to school when company is here."

With perfect, and yet, perhaps regrettable logic, Khalil replied, "Max doesn't have to go to school at all, but you do."

Olivia coughed and pretended to take interest in the contents of her breakfast plate, which held half of a blueberry muffin and a partial slice of bacon.

Her discretion went unnoticed. The storm broke. Chloe shouted, "Horrible! It's not fair that I have to go to school and he doesn't!"

The massive Djinn cocked his head as he regarded the small human girl in front of him. He asked gently, "Do you really wish to raise your voice to me?"

Olivia couldn't control her grin any longer. She picked up her coffee cup to hide behind it. Khalil was completely protective, unfailingly steady and truly loving with her friend Grace's niece and nephew, Chloe and Max. Otherwise his question might sound ominous, and she could see that it had thrown even Chloe off her stride.

The girl fell silent, frowning as she thought things over. Then she straightened her slender spine, tilted up her chin and said in a firm voice, "Yes."

"I believe you should take a few minutes to think about that, alone in your room," Khalil said. "Although I do admire your ability to pick a stance and stand by it. After ten minutes has passed, you will go to school as usual."

Chloe's mouth dropped open. She was the very picture of outrage. "Are you giving me a *time out*?"

Khalil snapped his fingers. "Ah yes, that is what it is called. A time out. I never remember, because it makes no sense. There is no such thing as a 'time out'. The time is the same in your bedroom as it is everywhere else in Florida."

A snort exploded out of Olivia before she could stop it. She clapped a hand over her mouth and managed to settle her coffee cup into the saucer before she spilled any of the hot liquid on herself.

Chloe wailed, her mouth open wide and delicate complexion turning pink. Blonde curly hair floating around her head like a halo, she turned to stomp down the hallway of Khalil and Grace's spacious, sprawling ranch home.

While Olivia watched her dramatic exit, Chloe almost ran into her aunt Grace, who limped toward the dining area with Max settled on her hip. Another Djinn, Khalil's daughter Phaedra, followed on Grace's heels.

As soon as Chloe saw the others, she wailed louder, dashed around them and disappeared, presumably to actually go to her room as she had been told. For such a strong-willed child, she was remarkably well behaved.

"Funny," remarked Grace. "I didn't hear any tornado sirens going off."

"Why would you hear a tornado siren?" Phaedra asked impatiently. "The sky outside is perfectly clear."

"I—you—never mind," Grace said. Olivia didn't bother to hide her grin any longer as Grace's dancing eyes met hers. Grace limped to the breakfast table, trailed by Phaedra. She announced, "Phaedra did quite well changing a diaper for her first time. And believe me, Max can produce some stinky diapers."

"Of course I did well," said Phaedra with a sharp frown. She crossed her arms. Her physical form stood taller than either Grace or Olivia, and she had chosen to appear in severe black clothing. Her white, regal features were very like her father's, while the straight fall of her shoulder-length hair was blood red, and black talons tipped her long fingers. "The contents of the diaper were remarkably unpleasant, so I simply stopped breathing until the end of the procedure."

"Yes, you did great," said Grace cheerfully. "In fact you did so well, I think you'll be ready to watch Max on your own in only sixteen or seventeen years."

"There, you see," said Phaedra as she turned to face her father. "Your concerns were for nothing."

Khalil's eyes narrowed and his expression turned guarded. He looked from his complacent, arrogant daughter to Grace's compressed, mischievous expression, then to Max. He opened his mouth and shut it again.

"Silence is a wise choice," Grace said to him. "She'll figure it out eventually."

Olivia burst out laughing. Exhausting though it could be, she loved this wacky household. It was completely different from her quiet life back in Louisville. Her job was demanding and she enjoyed her life, but the most exciting thing that happened in her house was when she gave catnip to her nine-year-old cat Brutus.

Khalil held his hands out for the baby. Max had jammed a forefinger up one round nostril. He stuck out his tongue and, grinning, blew a raspberry as Grace set him on his feet. Then Max high stepped his way over to Khalil, who swung the baby into the air and settled him in his lap.

Olivia noted fondly, and not for the first time, how much Max had changed in a year, but then they all had. Max was twenty months old, a healthy chunk of boy. At five years old, Chloe had started kindergarten, and normally she loved it, except when something exciting was happening at home.

But the biggest change Olivia saw was in Grace. The previous year, when she and Grace had become friends, Grace had been pale and tense, with shadowed eyes and lines of pain and exhaustion on her face. Grace was a good ten years younger than Olivia, but a year ago she had looked older.

Last year, Grace and her niece and nephew had lived in their old family home in Louisville, Kentucky. She had been recovering from the same car crash that had killed her sister and brother-in-law and left her with a permanent disability. She had also been struggling to come to terms with the Power of the Oracle, which she had inherited when her sister died, along with a mountain of debt.

Now Grace had regained her health. She would never lose the limp. Her knee had been too badly damaged, and at the time of the injury, she hadn't had access to high cost, premium magical health care. But despite that challenge, she looked happy, truly happy. The hollows in her face had filled out, and she was vibrant with color, with strawberry-blonde hair, sparkling hazel eyes and lightly suntanned skin.

By comparison, Olivia felt as if she looked like Grace's older, duller sister, with her short chestnut hair, gray eyes and pale skin that did not suntan well. It wasn't that she looked bad, she thought. All of her features were regular sized and in the right place, and while she had a sprinkle of freckles across her nose and cheekbones, they were acceptable enough. She just didn't look interesting, not like Grace's colorful, fiery blaze.

It seemed a metaphor for the difference in their lives. Even though she was young, Grace had already lived a life filled with heartache and drama, and she was involved with Khalil in a seriously smoldering love affair.

Olivia had lived a perfectly normal childhood. Her parents had paid for her to go to college. She did well, garnered some scholarships, studied magic, and directly out of school she had walked into an excellent job as a reference librarian at the Ex Libris Library in Louisville. There was nothing wrong with any of that, just as there was nothing wrong with her looks, except she had the nagging suspicion that she lived a boring life, and that she herself was a boring person.

Olivia didn't know all the details, but somehow Grace's troubled finances had smoothed out too. As Oracle, Grace had received a large cash contribution from a petitioner, and she received a regular monthly stipend from the new consulting agency that the Wyr gryphon Rune Ainissesthai and his Vampyre mate Carling Severan had established. All Olivia really knew was that Grace and the agency had worked out some kind of sliding scale fee system, so that she could still act as Oracle for those who did not have the ability to pay while the agency collected fees from those who could.

All of that translated into a sprawling ranch house on the beach, with a fenced in yard so the children could play in safety. And there was love in this house, so much love, Olivia felt privileged to witness it. Grace and

Khalil's relationship was so strong she could only imagine what it must be like to have such a relationship in her own life. They doted on the children, who thrived under such care. Their house seemed constantly full of Djinn, who either visited, brought gifts or bargained for healing that only Grace could give them.

Even Khalil's daughter Phaedra, while spiky and unpredictable, seemed to relax and enjoy the atmosphere and the children when she came to visit. Olivia wasn't sure what she thought about Phaedra, but at least the Djinn treated Max and Chloe with gentleness.

While Khalil bounced Max on his knee and Grace helped herself to breakfast, Olivia ate the last of her muffin. Phaedra stood nearby, her head cocked and diamond eyes piercing as she watched them.

Grace had told Olivia about the first time she had met Phaedra. Her eyes had been as black as twin oubliettes. The Djinn had been tortured and confined by her mother for so long, it had twisted her spirit. Now, thanks to the help that Grace had given her, her spirit was healed and straight again. But that didn't make her any easier to get along with.

Grace said to Phaedra, "You can sit down, you know. Eat something. Drink some coffee. Pretend to enjoy it, join in small talk."

Phaedra gave Grace a baffled, bored look. She said, "I have no interest in talking about little things."

"Oh, I don't know why I bother," Grace said. She turned to Olivia. "It's been so much fun to have you visit. I wish you could stay for longer than a week."

"I haven't enjoyed myself so much in years," Olivia told her. "Thank you for having me. I'm so glad you invited me for a visit before this new job starts."

"I'm just glad you could take the time," Grace said. "I'm going to miss you when you leave." She leaned forward. "Are you still excited? What am I saying, of *course* you're still excited."

"I can't wait." Olivia hesitated for a moment, then confessed, "I'm also really nervous."

Phaedra glided to the breakfast table, pulled out a chair and sat. Every move she made looked lethal and inhuman. "Why are you nervous?"

Olivia studied Phaedra, wondering what had sparked the Djinn's attention. Perhaps Phaedra was interested because she and Olivia were going on the same expedition.

Olivia explained. "I get to help pack and move one of the world's most legendary magical libraries, owned by one of the world's most legendary witches. This is a once in a lifetime experience. I wouldn't be surprised if every symbologist in the world had applied to go on this expedition, but only three were picked and I was one of them. That's exciting. It's also a bit nerve-wracking."

"Plus you get to hang out for a couple of weeks on a mysterious Other island," said Grace, grinning. "Well, at least it will be a couple of weeks according to island time. Who knows how long you'll be gone according to the rest of Earth. I wish cameras worked and you could take pictures."

Time and space had buckled when the world formed, creating pockets of Other lands where magic was stronger, the sun shone with a different light and time ran differently than it did on Earth. Often technology did not work, or it was downright dangerous. Sometimes the time slippage between an Other land and Earth was minor, and sometimes it was significant.

Olivia said, "When Carling hired me, she promised that the slippage wouldn't be any longer than a couple of months, if that."

Between Carling's assurance that the time slippage would be relatively minor and Olivia's promise to write at least two journal articles on the experience, she had been able to persuade the Dean of the library to approve a year's sabbatical so that she could make the trip and concentrate on writing about the experience afterward. Once she'd been hired and her trip had been approved, she'd been unable to sleep a full night since.

Khalil said, "Now, that is what I call a time out."

"Eeee," remarked Max. The baby sounded as if he agreed.

The remaining few hours of Olivia's visit flew by. A tear-stained Chloe gave her a big hug before drooping off to kindergarten.

Olivia watched her leave with a pang of regret. She may have decided not to have children of her own, but her decision wasn't based on health or financial reasons. She kept herself quite fit, and while she wasn't very tall, just barely topping five feet four inches, she had a constitution as sturdy as an ox.

As far as finances went, her profession was quite specialized. She was a witch working as a reference librarian at the largest library of magical works in the United States. Only skilled symbologists—those who were proficient at reading, controlling and infusing words and images with Power—could work at Ex Libris, and she was highly paid for what she did.

Not only did she own her house outright, but she also had a healthy savings account, a good stock portfolio and a pension that would allow her to retire early and in comfort, if she so chose.

She had just never found a steady, long-term relationship within which to consider having children, and though she was a human woman in her mid-thirties and her biological clock was ticking, she wasn't interested in having a child by herself.

After Chloe left for school, it was time for Max's morning nap. Olivia was happy to get one last chance to tuck him in his crib, then she and Grace talked for a few hours.

Olivia had already packed her bags, so when the time came to leave she only needed to collect her luggage from the guest bedroom. She had packed as her temporary employer, Carling Severan, had instructed, bringing one full-sized suitcase that could be left behind at either a hotel in San Francisco or a yacht in the Bay, and one water resistant pack that would carry all her essentials and clothing for the length of her stay on the island.

Taking the instructions as her cue, she had packed sensible, sturdy clothing that would be suitable for field work—jeans, T-shirts, sweaters, a wind-resistant raincoat, hiking boots and sneakers—along with a leather-bound journal for taking notes.

Mindful of the limited space in her pack, she kept her toiletries focused on the essentials, shampoo, soap, toothbrush, toothpaste and sunscreen, and she didn't bother to pack any makeup. That morning she wore jeans, a light blue, form-fitting T-shirt and sneakers.

Slinging the pack onto one shoulder, she wheeled the suitcase to the living room where Grace and Khalil stood with Max and Phaedra.

As Olivia appeared, Khalil was speaking to his daughter. "It is nonsensical to summon a taxi for Olivia when you are both traveling to the same place. You will transport Olivia and her luggage with you."

Phaedra appeared to have no problem whatsoever in facing down her formidable father. She said in a cold voice, "The only reason to transport a human anywhere is to use it as a means to acquire a favor."

Khalil said, "You have been away too long, either as a pariah with a bent spirit or resting in an incorporeal state. You are supposed to use this job as a means to reacquaint yourself with the world. Do not attempt to bargain with anyone on this trip. Listen to how people interact with each other, and learn from it. Do as Grace suggested. Make small talk. Don't kill anyone who does not deserve it."

Olivia raised her eyebrows. If ever there was an order based on too much subjectivity, that one was it.

Grace must have felt the same, because she murmured, "Khalil."

Khalil and Phaedra turned to Grace at the same time, their heads tilted in exactly the same way, imperious and inquiring. Grace said to Phaedra, "Don't kill anybody unless it is in self-defense. Period. Don't risk making a fatal mistake and possibly becoming a pariah again. You do not have the right to decide if someone else may live or die."

"I'll take that under advisement," Phaedra said, eyes narrowed.

Grace scowled and looked as if she would reply, but Olivia took that moment to step forward. "Excuse me," she said. "I need to call for a taxi if I'm going to make it to the agency offices in time for the meeting."

Khalil folded his arms and looked at his daughter. Phaedra's eyes narrowed further as she considered his expression. "Fine," she said between her teeth. "But only for the duration of this job." The younger Djinn turned to Olivia and gave her a razor sharp smile. "Come, human. We have a meeting to attend."

"Really, I don't mind calling a taxi," said Olivia. She would rather take a cab than get on Phaedra's bad side. She set her pack on the floor next to her suitcase and walked toward Grace, intending to hug her goodbye.

Phaedra's corporeal form dissolved into a whirlwind of Power that engulfed Olivia and yanked her away from the world.

A maelstrom surrounded her. There wasn't anything solid or stable anywhere. She wanted to scream, but some stubborn sense of pride made her swallow it down. She would not give the ornery Djinn the satisfaction of knowing that she had rattled her.

When the world re-formed, the details of her surroundings were completely different. Olivia stood in a polished hallway, outside double doors made from carved oak and propped open to reveal a conference room filled with several people.

Phaedra materialized beside her, long blood-red hair whipping around regal white features that were filled with subtle, smug amusement.

Everyone in the room turned to stare. They all wore different versions of the same kind of outfit Olivia wore, along with varying expressions of surprise.

Details blurred in the moment, except for a few standouts. Carling Severan, former Queen of the Nightkind, stood at the head of the conference table. She was a dark-haired, beautiful woman, with honey-colored skin and long, almond-shaped dark eyes.

Despite the fact that Olivia knew that Carling was one of the most Powerful witches in the world, and she was also one of the oldest and most Powerful Vampyres in the world, Olivia sensed no evidence whatsoever of the other woman's Power. The fact that Carling could cloak her Power to that extent was more than a little unsettling.

The Vampyre stood beside a man Olivia had never seen before. Both Carling and the man were the same height, which meant he could not be very tall, perhaps only a few inches taller than Olivia herself. He wore a plain gray T-shirt, jeans and boots, and he was extraordinarily striking, with a hard, boldly planed face half-hidden by sunglasses, short, dark brown hair speckled with flecks of white, and a palpable aura of power that was both physical and magical.

Along with everybody else, he seemed to be staring at Olivia and Phaedra. With his sunglasses, it was hard to tell where his eyes were trained, but at least his face was turned in their direction.

Olivia jerked her gaze away. She knew exactly what everybody was thinking. No one in her right mind would bargain away a costly, potentially dangerous favor in return for transportation from a Djinn, not for a trip that could be completed so easily by mundane means. Everyone present would think she was either insane, or insanely important.

Actually, scratch that thought. Nobody would believe she was insanely important.

There was probably a worse way to meet the people she would be working with for the next few weeks, but at the moment, she couldn't think of what it would be.

Olivia took a deep breath to try to calm her rioting nerves. Then she looked at the empty floor around her feet. Irritation took control of her mouth. She said to Phaedra, "You forgot my luggage, dimwit."

Realization transformed Phaedra's features, wiping the smugness away. The Djinn crossed her arms with a scowl. Then she blew into the whirlwind again. A moment later she reappeared, and Olivia's luggage landed with a thump at her feet.

The room was so silent, one could have heard a pin drop.

Let's be sensible, shall we? Let's not make an enemy of the whackadoodle Djinn.

"Thank you," she said, in as polite and dignified a tone as she could muster. Phaedra twitched a shoulder in impatient reply and stalked into the room to lean against a wall.

The tips of Olivia's ears felt as if they were burning, and so did her cheeks. She refused to look around at anybody. She especially did not look at the striking, powerful man who stood at the head of the room.

Instead, she picked up her suitcase and pack, carried them into the large conference room, set the pieces along the wall with the heaps of other luggage, and then sat at the large conference table, several seats away from anybody else.

The floor never did open up and swallow you, no matter how badly you might wish it.

Chapter Two

When nine people in total entered the conference room, Carling nodded to one of the men, who shut the double doors. The striking man in the sunglasses remained motionless beside the Vampyre, hands clasped behind his back. He appeared to be studying the occupants in the room, his strong features impassive.

Aside from Carling, there were four women and four men present. Two of the men were Wyr, including the man at Carling's side, and one male was an Elf. Olivia guessed that the fourth male was human. Of the other three women, there was one Djinn, of course, a Light Fae and a woman whose heritage and race Olivia couldn't quite place. Her coloring was similar to Carling's, her strong face attractively hawkish. She wasn't quite human. Olivia suspected that she was of a mixed race.

"Good afternoon," Carling said. "We have the agency plane waiting for you on the tarmac, so I will keep this meeting as short as possible. It is public knowledge that I have become estranged from one of my progeny, Julian Regillus, the Nightkind King. Julian and I are having several disagreements."

Several of the people sitting at the table exchanged glances. Carling and Julian's estrangement had, in fact, hit several major news websites and many tabloid sites, but Olivia could tell that nobody had expected Carling to speak so frankly.

Carling continued dryly, "The relevant disagreement today is regarding my library, which is located on a small island in an Other land that has a single underwater crossover passageway located in the ocean just outside the San Francisco Bay.

"I filed a suit with the Elder tribunal, which Julian countered with his own suit. I claim I have the right to retrieve my property, since it is located in a place outside of Julian's legal jurisdiction. Julian claims that he has banished me from the Nightkind demesne. Since the crossover passageway is located in his demesne, he has the right to bar access to me.

"My suit involved an offer of resolution where I would send a team that would travel to the island on my behalf. That team would pack my library and transfer it completely out of the Nightkind demesne. As some of you already know, the tribunal has granted my petition and ordered Julian to allow my team access to the harbor in order to transport my library. Upon completion of this task, I relinquish all rights and claim to the island. Since I also filed documentation about a sentient species that lives on the island, rights to that land will revert to them."

Carling turned to the man who stood beside her. "This is your expedition leader, Sebastian Hale. He has final say on all decisions. He has a full security team, most of whom will remain on board a yacht in the harbor. The three of his staff who will be traveling to the island are present here—Derrick, Tony and Bailey. Derrick is the medical doctor who will be traveling with the team."

Two men, the Elf and the human, and the Light Fae woman nodded to the group as Carling mentioned their names. Then Carling gestured to the hawk-faced woman of mixed race. "This is your head librarian and symbologist, Dendera Amin. Dendera is the department head for Magical Studies at the National Library of Turkey. She has final say regarding anything to do with the library itself. Her team has two other symbologists—Steve and Olivia."

The symbologists gave each other assessing looks and nods. Dendera's expression remained reserved, while Steve, a Wyr of some kind with a thin, intelligent face, gave Olivia a quick smile.

"Last," Carling said, "but certainly not least, there is one Djinn on the team, Phaedra, who will stand guard over the underwater crossover passageway while you are on the island. All of your resumes are on file with the tribunal. Phaedra, only these seven people are legally permitted to travel to the island. Certainly no Nightkind, nor anybody that Julian might suggest sending with you, should be allowed access. Julian will most likely keep a yacht in the harbor to make sure that we actually fulfill the terms of the petition.

"You have three days to make the crossover and start the removal process. If for any reason you fail to do so within that time frame, my petition becomes null and void, and I lose all legal claim to my library. It is Sebastian's job to see that this does not happen, and that you depart for the island well within that deadline."

The Vampyre paused to look at each one of them before she continued. "You're all excellent at your jobs, and that didn't happen by accident. I have been collecting that library for thousands of years. There are many items that are old, fragile, dangerous and valuable. Before I was forced to leave, I destroyed some of the darkest items, but I did not have time to safely contain or destroy everything. Stay on top of your game, be careful and work as a team. It's the responsibility of Sebastian and his team to safeguard both you and the contents of the library. Good journey and good luck."

With those final words, Carling strode out of the room, and Sebastian Hale faced the group alone.

"Dendera and I have already been thoroughly briefed," he said. His voice was as striking as the rest of him, strong and deep and rich. "I won't add anything else right now. We have several hours on the plane where we can get acquainted with each other and run through details of the expedition, so for now, get your luggage and make your way downstairs. There's transportation waiting to take us to the airport."

Phaedra pushed away from the wall. She looked bored again. She said in a curt voice to Sebastian, "I will see you in San Francisco after your flight."

Sebastian's hard face turned to the Djinn. "No, you won't. You will travel on the plane along with every other member of this crew."

Phaedra's expression turned edgy and unpredictable. "That's ridiculous."

"That's the rule," said Sebastian. "You travel with us and attend the meeting, or you're off the team. In fact, you do everything I say, or you're off the team."

The Djinn's expression turned deadly. "Don't push me, Wyr."

"Or you'll do what?" asked Sebastian, his voice flat. He tilted his head.

He looked unimpressed. Unafraid.

Which meant he believed he could face down a Djinn and win the confrontation.

Olivia was reluctantly impressed.

She also knew that Phaedra had already given her word to her father that she would see this assignment through successfully to its conclusion, so she was not quite as taken in by the scene as everyone else in the room.

She walked around the end of the table, collected her luggage and said to Phaedra, "Quit making an ass of yourself if you possibly can."

Then without waiting around for any more drama, she walked to the bank of elevators at the end of the hall.

One by one, other people joined her at the elevators. Olivia kept her head down and eyes to the floor. When the elevator doors opened, people filed in with their luggage. They rode down to the ground floor in silence.

Outside the main entrance, two black Cadillac Escalades idled at the curb. With a minimum of conversation, the group loaded into the vehicles. Olivia managed to score the front passenger seat of one Escalade. Thankfully neither Sebastian nor Phaedra joined the group in her SUV. During the trip to the airport, she listened to the others' desultory conversation from the back seat, but she didn't join in.

The driver took them to a smaller, more business-oriented airport than Miami International Airport, where Olivia had originally flown in. They met up with the group from the other Escalade, and in short order a uniformed flight crew took their luggage out to a corporate-sized Boeing parked on the tarmac. Soon after, the group filed into the sunshine to board the plane.

Sebastian went first. Olivia watched him run up the airstairs. It was such a simple, ordinary feat, running up stairs. But his body in movement was mesmerizing, full of grace and power, and so effortless he seemed to float. When he stopped in the doorway of the plane, she could hardly believe what she had seen. Watching him for those few seconds had taken her breath away.

He remained by the door, turning to watch the others as they boarded. When it came to her turn, she ducked her head as she climbed toward him and pretended she was invisible.

"You," he said when she reached the top.

Resigned, she lifted her head. She had been right about his height. He stood just a few inches taller than she did. His compact body was proportioned remarkably well, his shoulders not too wide, and his lean legs not too long. Exposed by the short sleeves of his gray T-shirt, his arms were cut with lean muscle.

Combined with his lack of expression, those sunglasses of his were truly unnerving. Up close, she felt the force of his presence as a palpable thing. As he turned his head to glance down the stairs at the others, she also saw that he was not as young as she had first thought. Lines bracketed his hard mouth and fanned out from the corners of his eyes. She couldn't tell if the white that flecked his sable brown hair so strikingly was from age, or if it was a characteristic of his kind of Wyr.

Groping for some measure of composure, she reminded him, "My name is Olivia Sutton."

"I know who you are," said Sebastian. He did not make that sound like a good thing. "Take one of the seats at the first table. You will sit with me."

Her entire body pulsed in reaction. Surprise, and something else, something quite out of the ordinary. All she knew was that her response was completely involuntary, and by the small tilt of his head, she realized he had sensed it. Damn those ultra-sensitive Wyr senses.

All the while, his expression remained as revealing as a stone wall.

She refused to feel as if she were back in grade school and summoned to the principal's office. With as much composure as she could muster, she said, "Certainly, if you wish it."

Without another word, he turned to the next person in line, and she knew that, at least for the moment, she had been dismissed.

Sebastian knew exactly when things had gotten interesting, and it hadn't been when he had accepted the contract for the job that Carling had offered and decided to head the team himself.

In fact, Bailey, his vice president and the second in command of his security company, had questioned that very decision at their home office in Jamaica.

"You're not cleared for work," she said, leaning her tall frame against the doorway of his office. Her sleek, Light Fae build was corded with muscle, and she kept her curling blonde hair cut short in a careless, charming tousle. "In fact, you're getting worse, not better. Why did you take this job?"

"There's no major, life-altering reason," he said without turning away from his desk. The morning had already turned sultry, and a ceiling fan pushed the hot air around the room. He had already discarded his shirt and wore cutoff jeans. He had promised himself a long, cool swim as soon as he had finished some necessary paperwork. "Carling is an old friend, and we bartered an exchange of services, that's all. And there's no point in me remaining holed up in this office, sitting on my ass while I wait for our research teams to bring me news of something that may or may not be of use to me. This way I can spend a few weeks keeping busy, while the time slippage will give them a few months to try to find answers."

Not that there was any real hope that any of their research teams would bring back something that could help him. He had not yet told Bailey what Carling had told him, gently, when he had consulted with her. He hadn't told anybody yet.

Bailey studied his expression. She didn't appear to like what she saw. "You sound so bored."

"I am bored," he told her. "I've been bored for a long time."

That had no doubt played a major factor in his getting injured during the last job, if "injured" was even the right word for what had happened to him. What was continuing to happen to him. He had made a huge mistake by underestimating the danger of the situation they had been in. He had been bored, and he hadn't been paying enough attention. He knew it, and Bailey knew it. Neither one of them said it aloud.

Instead, she said in a light tone of voice, "C'mon, it's an ancient, magical library on a deserted island that houses a mysterious sentient species. Aren't you the slightest bit interested in that?"

"Three months ago, I was protecting an archaeological party from a tribal chieftain who was in possession of a shrunken head that uttered curses against one's enemies." He shifted his sunglasses to rub his aching eyes. Another headache began to pulse in his frontal lobe. It would soon force him away from his desk, but he refused to give in to it just yet. "Five months before that, I was locating stolen gold treasure and transporting it back to the Thailand government, its rightful owner. Last year I was escorting a runaway Dark Fae heir back to his family in the Unseelie Court in Ireland."

He'd had decades of exotic experiences. He was drowning in exotic experiences. They all ran together in his mind like a never-ending banquet of highly seasoned, complex delicacies, and his palate had turned jaded.

When he had been a younger man, he could barely stay in one geographical location long enough to do the necessary paperwork to start a business. Now that he was no longer young, he was not interested in yet another astonishing adventure. He needed the good, solid nutrition of…something, but he didn't know what that something was.

"Then let me take care of the job with the magical library," Bailey said. "Carling didn't say that you had to be the one to do it personally, did she?"

He didn't reply, because actually Carling hadn't. She had just asked that his security company take on the contract.

Bailey read the answer in his silence. "Why don't you stay home? Better yet, take a vacation. Get laid, for God's sake. In fact, get laid a lot, and get drunk too. A lot. It would improve your disposition exponentially."

"Fuck off," he said.

"You fuck off."

He slammed both hands on his desk. "I'm not having a discussion with you about this. I've taken the job. I'm going. Deal with it and shut up."

He might not be interested in astonishing adventure, but he still had to keep moving, had to keep working. He couldn't give in to what was happening to him. If he gave in to it, it might kill him. Hell, it would probably kill him anyway.

On his last job, the tribal chieftain had died during the course of the struggle to gain control of the shrunken head, but not before he had used the head to utter one last curse against Sebastian.

According to Carling, the magic that had been unleashed had been precise and specific. The only way to free Sebastian from what was happening to him was if the chieftain who had cast the original spell used the shrunken head to lift the curse.

And that was impossible, because the bastard was dead. He glared at the shrunken head on his desk, currently being used as a paperweight, which was just about all it was good for, since neither he nor any of his company would ever use it to throw a curse.

He couldn't get rid of it. He needed it in case they found a way to break the curse without the chieftain's help. But as soon as he could, he was going to have it destroyed so nobody could use it again, and the poor, long dead bastard it belonged to would get some kind of final burial at last.

Bailey declared, "Well, if you're going on this job, I am too."

She knew as well as he did that they would make a lot more money if they each headed a crew and took separate assignments. Bailey was the very definition of mercenary, so if she volunteered to make less money and come along on the same job with him, it meant she was concerned. She wanted to watch his back, and that irritated him to no end.

He snapped, "I don't give a shit what you do."

"Keep it that way, asshole," she told him.

It was their little way of expressing affection for each other. He and Bailey had worked together for a very long time.

And the job remained just as he thought it would, mind numbingly routine.

Right up to the moment a human witch—a *librari-an*—appeared in a whirlwind of Power and called a Djinn a dimwit.

Witnessing that little scene was like having a switch thrown in his head. Just like that, after five years of a dangerous, growing ennui, he came back online, sharper and clearer than he had ever been. Engaged again. Interested.

Perhaps even amused, although he wasn't at all sure about that. After all, he had been stalled in a strange, restless kind of boredom for a long time.

Standing in the early afternoon Miami sunshine, he watched as the last of the group boarded the plane. Only then did he step inside himself. Leaving the crew to close and seal the plane door, he walked into the cabin.

The Boeing could seat up to eighteen people, so their crew had plenty of room to spread out. There were two couches set on either side of the cabin. Wide, comfortable chairs, all covered in elegant pale leather, were positioned in sets of four around tables. At the back of the plane, a complete, high-end galley could produce gourmet meals on long trips.

As soon as they were airborne and the plane had leveled out, everyone would be served their choice of filet mignon or grilled Dover sole, a fresh salad of mixed melon balls, balsamic braised asparagus, French rolls, and either chocolate mousse or a cheese plate with coffee for dessert.

When Carling had suggested the menu as a gesture of appreciation for their send-off, Sebastian hadn't objected. Soon enough the team would be eating rations that they carried in, fish that they caught and any vegetation they could harvest from the land.

The Djinn had chosen a seat at the back of the plane, and everyone else had given her as wide a berth as they could in such limited space.

As instructed, Olivia sat alone at the first table, opposite his laptop and files. He had studied her, at least as much as he was capable of, earlier in the conference room. Up close, he could take in all the details that he could no longer discern at a distance.

The sunshine slanting into the window brought out deep auburn glints in the chestnut-colored hair that lay in a sleek cap against her well-shaped head. While her blue T-shirt was plain, it fit snugly against her feminine figure, and the color was flattering to her pale, lightly freckled skin. She had intelligent gray eyes and a sensitive face, with shifts in expression that were subtle and nuanced. He could easily separate her feminine scent from the mélange of all the other scents in the cabin, and he found it delicious.

That reaction she'd had earlier—it had been an involuntary response. Her heart had pounded. He had seen the tiny flutter of pulse at her carotid artery. He was not sure what had prompted her reaction, and he found himself intrigued, even though she could have merely been surprised.

At the moment she looked calm, which he found irritating. She cradled a smartphone in small, capable-looking hands. At first he thought she was texting someone, but then he caught a glimpse of bright fruit exploding on the screen.

She played Fruit Ninja.

So much for his powers of intimidation. He refused to smile.

He had set his laptop and files in the seat that faced toward the back of the plane, so that he could assess various members of the group during the flight. Now he slid into his seat and buckled his seat belt.

She looked up quickly, switched off her phone and tucked it into a pocket, then buckled herself in too. Although her expression turned expectant, he didn't speak right away. The plane taxied onto a runway and prepared to take off. Another headache flared at the back of his eyes. He closed them, enduring the high, escalating whine of the plane and the thrust from the engines that sent them hurtling down the runway and pushing into the sky.

When he opened his eyes again, Olivia had turned her attention to the passing scenery outside the plane window. A frown had etched itself onto the delicate skin between her sleek brows. Now, instead of looking calm and composed, she appeared unsettled. Perhaps his prolonged silence bothered her.

He said to her telepathically, *I want some assurance that you and the Djinn are not going to cause me any problems on this trip. Convince me of that.*

Chapter Three

Olivia's attention snapped back to him, her eyes flaring with astonishment.

She said, *Excuse me?*

The headaches made him terse. He wanted to snap at everything and everyone in sight. Through an exercise in self-discipline, he managed to keep himself from biting her head off. *I want some assurance that you and the Djinn are not going to cause me any problems on this trip. You need to convince me of that.*

She raised her eyebrows, her expression turning cold. *Or what?*

He raised his eyebrows as well, mirroring her expression. *Or I will get rid of both of you and tell Carling that I need replacements.*

Her astonishment turned to anger. *My resume and recommendations speak for themselves. And why on earth would you presume that I could possibly predict what Phaedra may or may not choose to do?*

He crossed his arms and rested his aching head against the back of his seat. *Clearly you two know each other.*

Not that well, she said grimly.

I find that hard to believe, he said. *You were certainly close enough for her to transport you to the meeting, and for you to call her a dimwit and tell her not to make an ass of herself.*

Just like that, her quick anger faded to what seemed to be a mixture of embarrassment and exasperation. She heaved a sigh and pinched the bridge of her slender nose. *She made me angry, and it just fell out of my mouth.*

So the auburn glints in that sleek chestnut hair of hers indicated a temper. All right, perhaps now he was amused. Somewhat.

He said, his mental voice dry, *Do you often get angry at Djinn and tell them off without fear of repercussion?*

No, she told him emphatically. *In fact, I met Phaedra for the first time this week. Her father is in a relationship with a good friend of mine. Because of that connection, I've become one of Phaedra's associates by default. She wasn't supposed to transport me. I was going to take a taxi to the meeting. She did it to be irritating.* Her expression turned wry. *I'm pretty sure she won't zap me for calling her a dimwit. Grace would have something to say to Khalil about that. In spite of any possible evidence to the contrary, I think Phaedra cares what her father thinks.*

Various pieces of information fell into place. Grace Andreas was the Oracle, a position that came with an inherited Power, which was passed down from an ancient line of humans that could be traced all the way back to the Oracle of Delphi. The young Oracle's reputation was growing at a rapid pace. Recently she had become affiliated with Carling and Rune's consulting agency.

In fact, Carling had suggested that he petition the Oracle about the problem of his curse, but he had been too disheartened by their conversation to follow through with her advice.

He didn't see how a prophecy from the Oracle could help him. The Oracle could only tell him what he already knew, that he would become totally blind within the next twelve months if he didn't find some way to stop what was happening to him. He had sent a dozen teams into various parts of the world to try to find ways to break the goddamned curse, which, according to Carling, was a massively expensive, futile effort. But he could no longer leave any avenue unexplored, so he needed to consult with the Oracle as soon as he finished this latest expedition.

He set his own issues aside for the time being to consider what else he knew that was relevant to the success of this expedition. Djinn rarely became intimately involved with anyone outside their own race, and Grace's relationship with the Djinn Khalil of the House Marid had become famous.

And Sebastian had heard a thing or two about Khalil's daughter.

He frowned. *I do not understand what made Carling bargain away a favor for help from a Djinn who is reputed to be a pariah.*

Olivia's gaze fell. She appeared to concentrate on running a forefinger precisely along the edge of the table. His attention sharpened on the movement. Her fingernails were trimmed short, the nail bed of her forefinger a healthy pink.

He thought of her doing the exact same gesture, only this time running her finger down his bare skin. The skin along his back prickled lightly with goose bumps, and his breathing deepened.

He set his reaction aside and focused on what was relevant. *You know something about the bargain.*

She shook her head. *It's not my place to say anything. Anyway, it isn't any of our business.*

Everything to do with this expedition is my business, he told her. *You might as well tell me. Otherwise, I'll call Carling and ask her about it. She'll tell me everything I want to know, so don't waste my time.*

Her gaze lifted again, and the exasperation was back, only this time it was directed at him. All right, maybe he smiled at that. Just a little.

Carling didn't bargain away a favor for Phaedra's help, she said. *Khalil bargained away a favor to Carling to give Phaedra a job.*

Well, he hadn't seen that one coming. He let his head sag back against the seat rest as he muttered, "Fuck."

Hey, Olivia said. She leaned forward, looking earnest. *Give her a chance. I know she's not very likeable, and she certainly isn't housebroken. But Grace and Khalil have invested a lot in her rehabilitation, and Carling would never have agreed to the bargain if she thought Phaedra wouldn't hold up her end of things. Plus, she backed down when you confronted her. She's here on the plane, isn't she? That's because she made a promise to her father, and keeping her word matters to her. She's not a pariah. She'll do her job.*

He regarded her steadily, unconvinced. He was more than halfway inclined to boot Phaedra off the team and insist that Carling bargain for another Djinn to guard the passageway while they worked.

Then, suddenly curious, he asked, *Why does this matter so much to you? You certainly don't sound as if you like her much, yourself.*

She ran her fingers through her hair, clearly at a loss as to what to say. As he waited without prompting her, his gaze traveled down the angle of her neck, along the graceful arch of her collarbones, and farther down to the hint of cleavage at the scooped neckline of her shirt.

Something about her moved him. He could not figure out what it was. He'd always enjoyed women, and he had lost count of how many lovers he had taken by the time he was forty. Now he was over two hundred years old, and his species of Wyr did not live much past two hundred and fifty.

She was just another woman, like countless others. He knew without having ever seen them that her breasts would be charming, with either pink nipples or brown, and the indentation of her waist would fit perfectly underneath his hands. The skin at the back of her knees would taste delicate against his tongue, and her private flesh would be sumptuous, delightful.

None of that was surprising, and certainly none of it was original.

Perhaps what moved him was the composition of her curvaceous body against the straight architecture of the seat, or the contrast of how her pale skin looked dappled in shadow and the slanted sunlight from the nearby window. Or perhaps it was something different altogether, a secret of the spirit encased in her flesh. Or even her struggle to provide a thoughtful reply to his question. Perhaps it was simply her intelligence.

Then she dropped her hands from her hair and folded them on the table. Something coalesced in her, a decision or an understanding. She looked in the direction of his eyes, hidden behind his sunglasses. With her expression quiet and composed, she said, *Because she loves a couple of vulnerable human children. And because if I were deemed a lost cause, as she has been, I would want someone to fight for me.*

That was it, he thought. Whatever *that* was, encapsulated in the moment of decision and framed by her words.

That was what caught at him and held his interest, that intangible, ineffable thing.

During their telepathic conversation, the plane had finished its climb in altitude. The delicious smell of cooked food wafted from the galley. Sebastian unbuckled his seat belt and stood briefly to get everyone's attention.

He said, "We're going to eat lunch now, and after everybody has finished their meal, we'll have our meeting. We'll be busy when we hit the tarmac at SFO, so think of what questions you would like to ask now."

Olivia peered around the corner of her seat at the others while he spoke. She did not see much friendliness in the expressions of those that glanced at her. Between arriving in the midst of a very Djinn-like flourish, mouthing off more than once and now sitting with the expedition leader, it appeared that she had managed to alienate herself from just about everybody in the group.

Dendera spoke up. She had a light, sandy voice. "I want to meet with the other symbologists too."

Sebastian nodded. "We'll have time for that."

As Sebastian slid back into his seat, the flight attendant wheeled out a cart laden with their lunches. Olivia had chosen the Dover sole, while Sebastian had chosen both the sole and the filet. Apparently he was finished with their conversation, for he turned on his laptop and worked in silence while he ate.

She didn't mind. A little of his forceful presence went a long way. Even with the mental distance he set up between them, she was excruciatingly aware of every move he made, from his quick, decisive bites of food to the rapid typing on his keyboard. Once he shifted in his seat, and his jeans-clad calf brushed against hers. She felt as if he had stroked her naked leg with the palm of his hand. She shivered in reaction, and he seemed to pause what he was doing.

Of course that might have been totally in her imagination. He might have merely paused to read something on his laptop screen.

The fabulous meal was served with either a cabernet sauvignon or pinot grigio, and she was not a dainty eater.

She chose the white wine and consumed with enthusiasm everything that was put in front of her, down to the crusty French roll, which she smothered with the pat of organic butter.

Dessert was as delicious as the main meal had been, the chocolate mousse light, intensely rich and melting against her tongue, topped with a dollop of freshly whipped cream. The dark sweetness of the mousse was complemented perfectly by the bold taste of the French roast coffee.

After polishing off his steak and fish, Sebastian had chosen the cheese plate for dessert, not the sweet, and as she watched him eat out of the corner of her eye, she felt pretty certain that he was some kind of predator Wyr.

He never removed his sunglasses, not even to eat. She wondered why. He didn't exactly have a warm and approachable personality. Was it to keep a barrier between himself and others?

The atmosphere in the cabin had lightened with the wine and the excellent meal, and voices rose companionably. She smiled to herself as she listened. Their temporary employer had chosen a wise way to break the ice. The only person who had not appreciated lunch was Phaedra. When Olivia checked on the Djinn, she saw that Phaedra had slipped on a set of headphones and sat with her eyes closed.

Sebastian stood as soon as the attendant had cleared away their empty dessert dishes. He said without preamble, "Here are the next steps. The rest of my security team has already assembled in San Francisco.

They have been collecting all the supplies and equipment that we will need, and they will remain on watch on the yacht while we cross over."

"With time slippage, that could be a long spell for them," Dendera said.

"They'll follow a rotation for shore leave, and the yacht will dock periodically for fuel and supplies," Sebastian replied. "Meanwhile Phaedra will guard the crossover passageway itself. When we land, we will go directly to the yacht and spend the night on board. First thing in the morning we will make our first crossing. Because only eight of us are allowed to cross over, we'll have to make the trip several times with supplies. The same thing will be true when we transport the contents of the library."

The library would be transported in custom-designed, hermetically sealed containers. Sebastian passed around photos. Olivia studied them curiously when the Light Fae woman, Bailey, handed them to her. She couldn't imagine what the cost of the expedition was, with the legal battle, the highly specialized team, the security, the yacht, supplies and equipment, including wet suits and diving gear, and now these containers, but the running total had to be in the millions. Carling really wanted her property back, which did not surprise Olivia in the slightest, since the library itself had to be priceless.

After the question and answer session, Dendera stood and said to Olivia and Steve, "Let's meet at the empty table in the back. I'll be with you in just a few minutes."

Sebastian had sat down again. He didn't look up or otherwise acknowledge that Olivia left the table. Feeling oddly let down, she shrugged it off and moved to the back of the plane where Steve had already slid into a seat. She chose the one across the table from him. Dendera had disappeared in the direction of the lavatory, so at the moment she and Steve sat alone.

The other symbologist was tall, around six feet or so, with a lanky build and large, long-fingered hands. Trying to guess a Wyr's age without any knowledge of his animal form was an exercise in futility, but if Steve were a human male, she would have pegged him in his late thirties. His dark hair had receded somewhat from a high forehead, and he wore a speculative expression on his thin, rather bony face as he considered her.

How did your first meeting with his lordship go? Steve asked her telepathically. *Did he give you the same 'my way or the highway' speech that he gave the Djinn?*

Taken aback, Olivia said the first thing that popped into her head. *His lordship?*

You know what they say about short men and Napoleonic complexes, Steve told her. He glanced toward the head of the plane, his eyes filled with a sharp gleam and his expression cynical.

She had been so focused on how people would react to what she had done, she hadn't given a thought to how different someone else's perspective might be. And she was immediately convinced she did not want to have this talk with Steve.

She leaned back in her seat as if trying to put more distance between them, as she said cautiously, *I don't know what you mean.*

Steve might be intelligent, but he did not appear to pick up on her verbal or nonverbal cues. His lips twitched into a thin smile. *As soon as I heard that the great Sebastian Hale himself would be leading the expedition, I did a little more research on our fearless leader. He has quite the reputation for being aggressive and dictatorial. Just like I said, Napoleonic complex.*

The "great Sebastian Hale"?

What was great about him?

Don't ask. This conversation was a minefield. She rarely developed a dislike for someone as quickly as she did for this symbologist, and she fought again the impulse to squirm.

Steve looked at her expectantly. She wanted to stay silent and ignore him, but he was one of the two people she would be working with daily for the next few weeks, and she couldn't quite bring herself to shut him down so flagrantly.

Fumbling for a neutral, diplomatic response, she said, *I've never heard of him before. I didn't research anybody who came on the trip.*

Though she hadn't intended for him to, Steve took that as a request for more information. He said, *Hale runs one of the best security companies in the world. They're based in Jamaica. He won't have anything to do with Dragos or the Wyr demesne, but word is, he could have been a sentinel if he'd wanted to. He's supposed to be that good.*

There were seven demesnes of Elder Races in the United States—Wyr, Elven, Light Fae, Dark Fae, the Nightkind, Demonkind and the human witch demesne, which was based in Louisville, Kentucky.

Dragos Cuelebre, ancient dragon and multibillionaire, governed the Wyr demesne in New York. At the core of his governing structure were his seven sentinels who were reputed to be the strongest Wyr in the world. She didn't want to be impressed by anything Steve told her, but she couldn't help it. She glanced over her shoulder at where Sebastian sat, deep in his work. The hard planes of his face were as remote as ever.

Steve continued, *Not that Hale would be a suitable choice any longer as a sentinel in any case. As an owl shifter, his lifespan is only around two hundred and fifty years, and he's grown too old.* When she turned around to face the table, Steve's expression had turned calculating. *Of course, if his eyesight is so sensitive that he can't even take off his sunglasses in daylight that might have disqualified him too.*

But Steve was wrong about that. Despite popular belief, Olivia knew that owls could see perfectly well in daylight, and in fact their vision was extraordinary.

Sebastian wore his sunglasses for an entirely different reason. Not for the first time, she wondered why.

Chapter Four

Thankfully at that point, Dendera returned from the lavatory and put an end to Steve's unwelcome gossip. The three symbologists spent the next hour discussing how they would approach safely packing the most fragile items in the library, which included a rich collection of works on papyrus.

"Carling said she kept a handwritten catalogue of items in her office," Dendera told them. "Unfortunately, it's not based on a professional library catalogue system, but we're not to reorganize anything. Our job is to simply keep the collection structured the way it is, and make sure it's all packed properly. We also need to make sure that the magical works are safely contained, so that they don't cause damage to anyone when they're shifted."

When Olivia thought of the work ahead, her excitement rose all over again. As a private collection, not many people beyond Carling herself would have viewed the contents of the library. Perhaps assistants had gotten the opportunity through the centuries, or protégées that Carling might have taken on. This opportunity really was the chance of a lifetime. Of several lifetimes.

The rest of the day sped away in a flurry of activity. When the plane landed in SFO, more Cadillac Escalades were waiting to take the group to the Marina Yacht Harbor, just east of Chrissy Field and the Presidio, at the northernmost tip of the peninsula.

The private yacht was massive, with plenty of space in the cargo hold to transport the collection. As soon as Olivia saw it moored in its slip, her mental tally of the cost of the expedition shot higher. A crew of six waited on board for them, each one of them members of Sebastian's security company. From the snatches of conversation she overheard, apparently Sebastian owned the yacht—or at least his company did.

As soon as they boarded, Sebastian disappeared. Olivia found herself disturbed by how disappointed she was at his absence. She had all too quickly developed a fascination for him. Making a determined effort, she managed to banish him from her mind and concentrate on the tasks at hand.

The crew showed the newcomers to their tiny cabins, which were little more than glorified closets with bunk beds built into the walls. Olivia and Dendera were to share one cabin.

She didn't mind the lack of space or privacy. They would only spend one night on the yacht and cross over the passageway first thing in the morning. After they had finished on the island and the library was safely stored in the cargo hold, the yacht would set sail for international waters, at which point Carling could take possession of the library personally, while Olivia and the others could fly home.

They checked food supplies and containers, tried on wet suits to make sure of their fit and ran through the procedure for crossing over. All members of Sebastian's team were experienced scuba divers. Dendera, Steve and Olivia were not, and they would use a buddy system for the crossover itself. Each of the three symbologists would make the journey with one of the security team. After the run-through a nearby restaurant delivered supper, which was a simple fare of deli sandwiches and potato salad, along with a yeasty, golden beer from a local microbrewery.

Finally, around nine thirty, Bailey, who had assumed command in Sebastian's absence, declared that they were done for the day. Everything was packed with precision, and all the equipment had been double-checked. Bailey gave permission for shore leave for what remained of the evening.

Steve, Dendera and half of the security crew disembarked, while the other half remained on duty. Phaedra disappeared too, although Olivia could still sense her presence. She thought the Djinn had not actually left the yacht but instead had merely chosen to let go of her physical form. Olivia couldn't know for sure, but she guessed that the Djinn had dematerialized to avoid any more need to socialize.

Having no interest in exploring the San Francisco nightlife, Olivia chose to remain aboard. Her body clock was acclimated to Eastern Standard Time and insisted it was past midnight. She was both tired and wound up.

Unwilling to crawl into her cramped bunk, she pulled on a sweater and her jacket and took a second bottle of beer with her up to the deck. Within a few moments, she was shivering. She had packed with the island weather in mind, which, Carling had informed her, was consistently mild. The bottle of beer, while excellent, was chilled, and a frigid wind blew off the Bay and pierced through all of her clothing.

But the view was so stunning it held her at the rail. The illuminated Golden Gate Bridge arched high over silver-tipped, black water. Traffic wound along the bridge in a long, undulating ribbon of incandescence. Lights blazed everywhere on both sides of the Bay underneath a night sky draped with moody clouds. She could feel the magic of the Other land shimmering in the distance, and she was so happy to be exactly where she was in that moment, all of her senses were wide open.

She felt Sebastian's forceful presence a moment before a wool blanket settled around her shoulders. He moved to stand at the rail beside her, and she grabbed at the edges of the blanket before it could slip to the deck.

He asked, "You weren't interested in going into the city with the others?"

"Not in the slightest," she said. She made a conscious effort to relax her jaw so that her teeth wouldn't chatter. "Especially not when there is a breathtaking view like this one. Thank you."

"You're welcome. When you're through with the blanket, you can fold it up and put it back in the storage box."

She looked where he pointed at an oblong white container set in the shadows behind a steeply slanted ladder that led to the pilot's cabin. Then she glanced back at him. He had slipped on a worn leather jacket but hadn't bothered to zip it closed. Underneath he wore the same gray T-shirt that he had earlier, the thin material molding against his muscled chest and flat abdomen, yet he appeared perfectly comfortable in the chilly night.

He still wore his sunglasses. As certainty settled into place, she felt an unexpected pang. She had seen him do any manner of tasks that said he was sighted, such as reading off his laptop, but something must be wrong with his eyes.

She turned to face the water, pulled the blanket tighter around her and said, "It's so beautiful out here, I don't want to go in."

He stayed silent for so long, she began to wonder if he was through interacting with her. When he finally replied, he sounded reluctant, almost as if he spoke against his better judgment. "There are deck chairs in storage too, if you want."

She decided she was being too fanciful. After all, he didn't have any reason not to speak with her, and he had, after all, been the one who approached her with the blanket.

She gave him a sidelong smile. "Would it be too odd for me to huddle under blankets and sleep on the deck all night?"

His hard-planed face turned toward her. "I have done so many times."

Her smile turned wistful. "How lovely. I imagine you've traveled all over the world."

"I've spent most of my life traveling for one reason or another."

Even though she barely knew him, once again she heard layers of nuance in his voice. Not regret, necessarily, but some emotion close to it.

He shifted into a more casual stance and rested his weight on both hands as he gripped the railing. Surreptitiously, out of the corner of her eye, she studied the hand that rested closest to hers. It looked strong and as beautifully proportioned as the rest of his body, broad, with long fingers, and a tracery of veins along the back.

"I like home life, and I like to nest," she said. "I don't think I would be happy living a life like yours, but it's fun to hear stories and to daydream."

"It gets tiring," he said. "You can have too much of any one thing, and then it all runs together into sameness."

Ah, she recognized the emotion in his voice. Resignation.

"I think so too, which is why I want to make a point of traveling a bit more. I don't want to look back on my life and have any regrets."

"Good for you," he said. His head turned as he looked out over the rippling water of the Bay. "You should make a point of doing things that you want to do. Regrets can be a bitch."

She remembered her bottle of beer, finished the last few swallows and set the empty bottle at her feet to dispose of later. Then, because he seemed halfway approachable, and she enjoyed standing beside him and talking, she confessed, "I've been so excited at this trip, I don't think I've slept a full night in months. As much as I love my job, I spend most of my life in a library. I've never traveled down a crossover passage or been to an Other land."

He turned back to her, frowning slightly. "If I recall correctly, none of you have much experience scuba diving."

She knew he was talking about all the symbologists, because his crew was highly trained for everything they needed to do. He hadn't been present for any of the evening's activities, so either Bailey had briefed him or he remembered that detail from their individual files.

She said, "That's right. I went into a practice tank a couple of times to get ready for the trip, but I've never actually been diving."

His frown deepened. "It's too bad that this will be your first time for both diving and crossovers. They can both be terrific experiences, but I don't think you'll be getting the best of either this time around. Travelling underwater through the passageway will probably be disorienting. It'll be dark, and the magic will shift as you travel. You might find it uncomfortable."

Bailey had said the same thing earlier. Olivia shrugged. "I'm not claustrophobic, and I think the buddy system for the crossing is a good one. And the actual underwater trip isn't supposed to last long. This trip is more than worth a brief amount of discomfort."

He turned to lean back against the railing, arms crossed. He said, "I'll partner with you for the crossover."

Once again she reacted physically, as surprise throbbed through her.

Surprise, and something else.

They would be swimming together in dark water with magic swirling all around them. She thought of his forceful, steady presence alongside hers. His hard, powerful body would move through the water with the same effortless grace he had bounded up the stairs with before. Her mouth went dry.

She managed to clamp down on the, "Yes, please," that was ricocheting around in her head. Instead, more or less calmly, she replied, "Thank you."

And, damn him, he picked up on her reaction for a second time, despite the wind blowing off the Bay and the indirect lighting from the yacht and the lampposts that dotted the length of the slip.

His attention sharpened on her. She could see it in the shift of his expression, and the change in his body stance. His already forceful presence became so intense she could not take a steady breath. It shuddered out of her, another telltale reaction.

She did not feel that she was in control of her own body.

He was.

He pulled this response out of her without ever touching her.

Her composure started a long, slow slide down an unknown hill, to an unseen destination. Still facing the railing, she leaned against it to steady herself as she huddled in her blanket, averted her gaze and pretended to look out over the water. Every nerve in her body turned on until she felt ablaze with some kind of light.

In a liquid glide filled with predatory grace, he turned fully toward her and moved closer until he stood at her shoulder, and a shiver ran along her skin. Angling his head, he pushed into her personal space. Not much, not so that their bodies touched, but just enough.

Speaking quietly, almost in a whisper, he asked, "Are you warm enough now?"

The warmth of his breath curled against her chilled cheek, and her shivering turned convulsive.

This was a man who knew exactly what he was doing, each movement choreographed down to the millimeter. That should have turned her off. It always had before. But it didn't this time. Where was her turn off switch?

With lightning speed, her mind tried out and discarded several answers in an effort to find one that sounded normal. The problem was, they all sounded suggestive.

I'm warm enough now. Oh, thank you. (*Don't even.*)

I could be warmer. (*No. It doesn't matter if it's the truth. Just NO.*)

The decision was too difficult. She couldn't figure out what to say, and the mounting pressure of the passing seconds got to her. She muttered, "I—I don't know."

His hand clamped down on her shoulder, the grip punishingly tight. It jolted her so much, she jerked her head up and stared at him.

He wasn't looking at her. His attention had turned to the dock. She looked in the same direction.

Several Nightkind creatures walked toward the slip where the yacht was moored, including two trolls, four ghouls and five Vampyres. Ten of the Nightkind, including the trolls, wore black Nightkind uniforms. The last of the Nightkind strode at the head of the group.

Even for someone like Olivia, who did not live or socialize in elevated circles, he was a very recognizable Vampyre. He wore tailored evening clothes that fit his tall, powerful frame superbly. He had short black hair that was streaked at the temples with flecks of white, a rough-hewn, aquiline face and a piercing, wolfish gaze.

Julian Regillus, the Nightkind King himself, had come to pay them a visit.

Sebastian's hand on Olivia's shoulder remained a heavy, hard presence. She could feel pressure from every one of his fingers, although when she glanced at his face, he looked expressionless.

Two of the security crew on duty stepped out of the pilot's cabin, their faces sharp. They froze when Sebastian gestured to them. He said nothing, but just watched as the Nightkind King and his group approached until they stood at the foot of the boarding ramp.

The King looked up at them where they stood at the railing, his hands on his hips, while his people fanned out around him. From what Olivia understood from popular media, Carling had turned Julian at the height of the Roman Empire. Julian had been one of Emperor Hadrian's most famous and distinguished generals, and now he was one of the most ancient Vampyres in the world. Even from that distance, Olivia felt his Power covering the dock in a dark, seductive mantle.

Julian's gaze met hers and held it as effortlessly as if he cradled a glass of wine in his long fingers. What an incredible experience it would be, she thought, to talk with the Nightkind King. The things he had experienced, the vast amount of history he would remember… Although he had begun his life as a human, that was so very long ago, now he must be as different from humankind as all but the most alien of the Elder Races.

The King smiled slightly, almost as if he could read her thoughts. Life as a human had not been kind to him. It had etched itself across the rough planes and hollows of his face until he had conquered it. She wondered what tales the marks on his face told, the enemies he had fought, the pain he had endured, the victories he had won.

What would he confess to her as they talked into the night? Could she unlock the secrets of his soul, sprawled on velvet couches in front of a fire?

He was so strong yet so alone, and he needed her. She could sustain him, while he could fulfill her. Only him, only her, as the unending night scrolled on and on…

A snarl sounded beside her, the sound so violent and shocking it made her jump. She felt so disoriented, at first she could not make sense of what she heard, or why the velvet couches had vanished.

"*Stop it,*" Sebastian hissed between his teeth.

Olivia twisted to face the man beside her. Sebastian stared down at the King. His bold, hard face had transformed into a look of such naked aggression, she would have taken several steps back had he not held her anchored at his side with that iron, unyielding grip. His Power had roused as well, and surrounded her in sharp, invisible blades.

"I have not done anything," the King said. His smile had widened, not unpleasantly. "She is human. Some humans react this way."

While he spoke aloud, the darkest of voices came into her head. *If there comes a time when you wish to do so, you may come to me.*

And the thing that terrified her most was not that the King had issued the invitation, but that a wild desire had risen up inside of her in response to it. Shaking violently, she turned to face Sebastian and grabbed his T-shirt with both fists. He put his arms around her, his grip as hard and unyielding as his hand on her shoulder had been.

"Don't look at him," he muttered.

She nodded jerkily. She whispered, "I'm sorry."

"Don't be. It's not your fault."

As they spoke, she felt Phaedra's presence rouse.

Oh no, *no*.

This strange, deadly scene already had a dangerous unpredictability. They needed Phaedra's involvement in it like they needed extra holes drilled in their heads.

But something about the confrontation had triggered the Djinn's interest, and one of the unfortunate realities of this trip was that Phaedra definitely had a mind of her own.

Olivia dared to peek in the direction of the dock, although she tried not to look at Julian directly. Black smoke poured down the bottom of the boat ramp. Phaedra's physical form coalesced in front of Julian and the other Nightkind.

The Djinn stood directly in front of the Vampyre, her arms crossed, with long black talons laid along her biceps, deliberately on display. She had chosen to appear in her usual black, with her sleek fall of hair ruby-colored like blood, and her white, regal features wearing a haughty expression. The boat ramp was some distance down the length of the yacht, and Olivia could only see her profile, but as Phaedra glanced back up at Olivia and Sebastian, her eyes burned hot like stars.

Julian cocked his head as he regarded the Djinn, his expression sparking with something other than amusement. Every Nightkind creature surrounding him drew closer, and the atmosphere turned deadly.

In the iciest tone Olivia had ever heard from her, Phaedra said, "Vampyre, this female human is one of my associates, and she is under my protection. Do not meet her gaze. Do not speak to her, physically or telepathically. Do I make myself clear?"

Julian blurred into movement that was too fast for Olivia's human eyes, and so did Phaedra. When they stilled again, the Nightkind King held the Djinn with one powerful hand wrapped around her throat.

And Phaedra held him, too, with one of her hands wrapped around his throat. Olivia could see that her black talons had sunk into his skin. Vampyre blood trickled from the small puncture wounds. She thought of all the Vampyre groupies, nicknamed bottom feeders, who would pay a fortune for that tiny, precious trickle of the Nightkind King's potent blood.

"Now this has become an interesting evening," said Julian. His rough, aquiline face had turned brutal. He and Phaedra stared at each other down the lengths of their arms.

Olivia groaned under her breath. "This has become a disaster."

"It's perfect," said Sebastian.

Chapter Five

In just a few moments, Phaedra had affirmed her worth in Sebastian's eyes and justified his decision in keeping her on the team. As far as he was concerned, she and the Vampyre could tear each other into pieces. Then he could call the Elder tribunal, rightfully claim he had nothing to do with any of it, and they could all sit back in comfort to watch somebody else clean up the mess.

In the meantime, hoping that Bailey was within telepathic range, he said, *Where are you?*

Bailey said, *I'm in my bunk. What's up?*

He didn't waste time on details. *Call everybody who left for shore leave. Tell them to haul their asses back to the ship now. No excuses.*

Bailey's telepathic voice turned crisp. *You got it. Where are you?*

On deck. Julian's here.

Do you need me there?

I'll let you know. Stay put for now.

Huddled into his chest, Olivia still trembled in his arms. He glanced at her, and something powerful and violent surged up inside him at the expression on her tense, pale face. She looked shell-shocked and very frightened.

"It's all right," he whispered. "You're all right."

"I don't feel all right," she confessed. Her fists remained clenched in his T-shirt. "I really want to go to him. I don't, but I do."

"Dammit," he muttered. He wanted to punch something. Someone. He tightened his arms around her.

And somehow, in spite of all that, he liked the fact that she had reached for him when she needed to, and that she still held on to him.

He was a dickhead.

On the dock, Julian and Phaedra remained locked in their standoff, their individual Powers clashing like thunder against Sebastian's magical senses.

This time when Julian smiled, it was like watching a sword being drawn. "Our Power is designed to draw and trap our prey," he said. "In a few of us, the trait develops quite significantly as we age. You cannot dematerialize when I have a hold on you, Djinn."

Phaedra's expression never changed, and she gave back to the Nightkind King hardness for hardness, blade for blade.

She told him, "I have no intention of dematerializing. I am not, nor will I ever be, your prey. Leave the human alone, explain your presence and then leave."

Eyes glowing red, one of the ghouls hissed, "How dare you lay hands upon our King and speak to him in such a fashion?"

Sebastian wasn't very good at distinguishing individual features among ghouls, but he thought this one was female, and she wore the uniform of a captain. The ghoul prowled forward, followed by the other Nightkind, closing in on Phaedra and Julian.

The Djinn's eyes went supernova, blazing as bright as any other beacon in the night. She said, "You would be wise to listen to me. My grandfather is Soren, first generation Djinn and head of the Elder tribunal. My father is Khalil, prince of the House Marid, the strongest of all five of the Djinn Houses. Do you really want to make war upon me and my associations?"

Sebastian almost wished he had a bowl of popcorn. He could watch the shit they threw down all night. But Olivia's distress was deep and genuine, and nothing of what had just happened had anything to do with the job he had promised Carling that he would do.

He rubbed Olivia's arms as he raised his voice. "Phaedra, back down."

The Djinn's attention snapped to him, her eyes glowing like lampposts. Clearly not happy at the order, she scowled. Then she snapped open the fingers she had closed around Julian's throat, displayed her flattened hand in front of Julian's face and pulled it away.

She had no shortage of attitude. Sebastian would give her that. Phaedra was definitely a loose cannon and, as Olivia said, she was clearly not housebroken, but he liked her more now than he had before.

He turned his attention to Julian. "Please unhand my Djinn."

Julian cocked his head to one side as he contemplated Phaedra. "I'll get my hands on you again one day."

She smiled at him. The expression was a remarkably nasty one, a mere widening of the lips on a very cold face. "When that happens," she said, "I will not be bound by my word to obey someone else. Then we will see what comes next, Vampyre."

Julian did not just let go of Phaedra. He shoved her hard. Her physical form flew back in the air, but before she could impact the hull of the yacht, she dissipated in a swirl of black smoke.

When Julian turned to look up at them again, Olivia flinched away, averting her head to focus her attention on the body of the yacht. Sebastian felt again that wild, violent upsurge of emotion, a combination of fury at Julian for frightening her so much and the very real desire to do him damage.

He said through his teeth, "I take it that you had some point in coming here tonight."

"Yes, I did," said Julian. "I know that most of your crew are enjoying the many fine things my city has to offer, at places like the Rockit Room, the Red Devil Lounge, the Club Deluxe and the Hemlock Tavern."

Sebastian went rigid. Julian had specific locations on every one in his crew. When the Nightkind had arrived, Sebastian had taken note that Xavier del Torro, Julian's second, was absent from the group. Now he thought he knew why. Julian had his crew followed.

Bailey, he said. *Did you get through to everyone?*

Just finished calling, she said. *They said they would return ASAP.*

They would, if Julian allowed them to.

"What do you want?" he snapped.

Once Phaedra had dematerialized, the Nightkind King's attendants had relaxed. Julian slipped his hands into his pockets and turned to stroll along the slip closer to Sebastian and Olivia.

Julian said, "Usually the Elder tribunal is careful to close loopholes and contain all contingencies, but occasionally their edicts hold certain omissions. Here is a case in point. If your crew does not make the initial crossover within three—well, now it is nearing two—days Carling loses all rights to any of her property on the island. That deadline is non-negotiable. There is no provision for you being unavoidably detained. For example, the police can take your crew in for questioning in relation to various crimes that have occurred in the city this evening. They can detain them for up to forty-eight hours without booking them."

Sebastian very gently let go of Olivia to face Julian. He gripped the railing with both hands, struggling with the desire to throttle the Nightkind King himself. He growled, "Why the *fuck* would you do that? Are you that petty?"

At his angry words, a couple of the ghouls snarled and stepped forward.

Julian waved them back, and said, "Actually, I have no desire to do that." He stood in a casual stance, hands still in his pockets as he tilted his head back to stare up at

Sebastian. "Carling has invested a lot of time and energy into collecting that library over the centuries, and I don't care if she retrieves it. I do care about making sure she hasn't used retrieving the library as an excuse to implement some other agenda in my demesne."

"For God's sake, like what?"

"I don't know. But if you think she is not capable of such subterfuge, you don't know Carling at all." Julian pulled his hands out of his pockets. "So here is the deal. I am going to search your yacht quite thoroughly, and you are going to let me. Of course, if you choose not to allow it, I won't be able to promise that your people will make it back in time to make the deadline."

Sebastian clenched his hands on the railing so tightly, his fingers went numb. He forced himself to take deep, even breaths. Olivia put a hand on his back. He didn't know her well enough to interpret what she was trying to communicate, but her touch had the odd effect of calming him down. Just a little.

"Fine," he said. "On one condition."

Julian's people were so confident they had already started forward, which infuriated him, but they stopped again almost immediately.

Julian raised his eyebrows. "And that is?"

"You do exactly what Phaedra said," Sebastian told him, his voice clipped. "You do not meet this woman's eyes." He pointed at Olivia. He didn't care if it sounded or appeared rude. Olivia was already vulnerable to Julian, and Sebastian would be damned if he made that worse by giving Julian her name. "You do not talk to her. Not physically. Not telepathically."

"Well," said Julian. The King's voice had turned wry. "At least I can promise that I won't talk to her any more than I already have."

A half an hour later, a raging Sebastian paced in his cabin.

His room was easily three times the size of the others, with a wide cabin window, a double bed that he could fold up against the wall when he wanted to, and a desk that was built into the other wall. Still, he could only get a good five paces in before he had to whirl around and return.

The Nightkind guards had searched his cabin first with an insulting thoroughness. Now Olivia sat in the chair at his desk while they searched the rest of the yacht and Bailey dealt with them on her own.

Phaedra surrounded the cabin with her presence, filtering out all evidence of Julian's presence and sealing Olivia and Sebastian inside a protective bubble. The Djinn's presence felt heavy and sullen against his senses and did something weird to the air pressure in the room. He kept expecting his ears to pop.

None of the crew who had gone out that evening had returned yet.

"Goddamn bastards," he muttered under his breath. "They could do this for the rest of the night." For the next two nights. He had kept his word, but that didn't mean that Julian would. If Carling was capable of deceit and subterfuge, so too was her errant progeny. "Tell me again what he said to you."

"I've already told you three times. He said I could go to him if I wished. That's all."

But if she was still under Julian's thrall, was she telling the truth?

He glanced at Olivia and caught her surreptitiously wiping at her eyes with her head bent. That stopped him in his tracks. He strode over to squat in front of her. "Are you all right?"

She turned her face away and said, "Of course I am."

She lied with such composure and dignity, it blew apart all of his rage. He took hold of her chin and turned her face gently back to him.

Tears swam in her eyes.

He took a deep breath. His voice calm and quiet, he said, "Let's try that again. I will ask, 'Are you all right?' And this time you will tell me the truth."

"I feel humiliated," she said, very low. "I'm supposed to be intelligent. I'm very well educated. I am really good at my job."

"You are superb at your job. I don't have to see you in action to know that. You wouldn't be on this trip otherwise." He took both her hands. She still felt chilled. He cupped them between his own, trying to warm them up. "And so?"

"I thought I was a strong person," she began. "I've never had such a reaction to a Vampyre before, and I've encountered them countless times. I've helped dozens of them at the library without a single problem…"

"Stop," he said. "Just stop."

She fell silent and regarded him gravely.

"What happened is not your fault," he said. Her fingers moved underneath his. He realized he was crushing her hands between his and made a conscious effort to loosen his grip. "It has no bearing on your intelligence or your worth, or strength as a human. It's like—like coming down with cancer, or—" He cast about his mind for another example but came up blank, so he reached for something that he was more familiar with. "Or mortality. It's a part of your human condition. That's all. He is a very old, very Powerful predator, and you are his prey. Everything about him is designed to pull you in, and you heard what he said. Sometimes it takes humans that way."

She nodded and straightened her back. "Intellectually, I understand what you're saying. It's just taking my emotions a little while to catch up. You know, it's quite terrifying to not be in control of what is happening to you."

Her words hit him hard, and it was his turn to avert his face. He muttered, very low, "I know."

There was a pause. He could feel her gaze upon him almost like a physical caress. "That's happened to you too."

He didn't have to tell her anything. The thought flashed through his mind, and he even paused to consider it. He had no business opening up to someone like her, or attempting to develop a real connection. They lived vastly different lives, and his was cursed.

But that intangible thing about her still drew him, just as it had on the plane and earlier on the deck when they had talked. And he discovered that he wanted to confide in her.

His mouth twisted. He said, "It's happening to me right now."

Her hands turned under his, slender fingers closing around his. "What do you mean?"

Slowly he disengaged one hand, removed his sunglasses and looked at her. Funny how quickly the glasses had become such an ingrained habit that he felt naked and vulnerable without them.

Her breath caught, the tiny sound quite audible in the deadened quiet of the cabin. Then she leaned forward and cupped his cheeks between her hands as she stared at his eyes. He knew what she saw. He looked at the same thing several times a day.

He was an Eagle Owl in his Wyr form, the largest species of owl in the world, and normally his eyes were very like his Wyr form's, a kind of golden amber with an orange hue. The strange, brilliant color unsettled many people.

Now his eyes were changing. Darkness like spilled ink grew over the irises, the pupils and the whites. He had already lost some of his distance and peripheral vision. Eventually the black would take over completely.

"What happened?" she breathed. She stroked his temple. The caress felt shockingly intimate and kind, and it woke an immense hunger inside of him.

His voice turned harsh. "I'm going blind," he said. "The last job I took, I was guarding an archaeological party that traveled along the Amazon River. We were attacked."

He told her about the chieftain, the shrunken head and the curse, while horror and compassion shadowed her face. "We did everything to try to avoid actual violence, but there comes a point when you have to stop talking and fight for your lives. I think he wanted to strike me blind instantly so that I would be crippled in battle, but my body's natural immune system took over and started fighting it off. I get periodic headaches and low grade fevers. Eventually the curse will take hold completely."

She asked gently, "Isn't there some way to break it? Most written curses I've seen are structured like a lock and key. Verbal ones have to have the same kind of structure."

"This one has a very tight lock," he said. "I've expended most of the company's personnel and financial resources looking for a cure. In fact, I have a dozen teams searching in the field right now. Carling thinks the only way to reverse the spell is to have the chieftain use the head again. But of course that's impossible, because he's dead."

She shook her head. "There has to be something, some other way."

"Carling said I should consult with the Oracle about it," he said. "I don't think a prophecy will be much use, but I'll try anything. I plan on going to see her when we get back."

"Don't write off what Grace might be able to do for you," she said, still stroking his temple. "She's done some strange and wonderful things."

The disappointments of the last several months had been so bitter and extreme that a resurgence of hope hurt. His chest felt full of ground glass. He couldn't trust himself to say anything. Instead he gritted his teeth and merely nodded.

When she sat back and let her hands fall to her lap, he missed her touch.

Then he decided he wasn't going to miss anything. Not a thing. He would grab at every last bit of life, experience everything, take everything he wanted. He knew it was a selfish decision, and he didn't care.

No regrets.

He stood, pulled her upright with him and drew her into his arms. She came readily, wrapping her arms around his waist and resting her head on his shoulder. More shock shuddered through him at the rightness of it. They fit, hip to hip and shoulder to shoulder. She was more slender. He stood a little taller. Balance and counterbalance, like a lock and a key.

He ran his fingers through her short, soft hair, and she rubbed her hands up and down his back. "I just don't understand how somebody could do that," she whispered. "How they could throw a curse at someone and know it will destroy their life."

He could do that, throw a curse and destroy someone else's life. Or wield a weapon, or strike with his body. He could kill someone. He had, many times before.

"I came to realize a long time ago that there are two kinds of people in the world. There are those who are wicked, and those who are not." Julian. Phaedra. So many others he had met throughout his life. "And you are not one of them."

Sometimes it was a relief to close his damned eyes and exist in complete darkness. He did so and turned his face into her soft hair. She smelled unique.

He had been an idiot earlier. Of course her scent, her body, was surprising and completely original.

I'm going to take you, he thought. I'm going to take you even though it's selfish, and I'm going blind, and even when I shouldn't, because I want you too much not to.

Because he was one of the wicked.

Chapter Six

The protective bubble that Phaedra had drawn around Sebastian's cabin popped, and a few moments later Bailey pounded twice on the door.

"They're finally gone," Bailey called through the barrier. "The fucking fuckers."

Sebastian raised his voice, the deep timbre vibrating against Olivia's cheek. "It's about time. I'll be right out."

Olivia wasn't ready to let go of him. The hard length of his body against hers, the feel of his arms around her, all answered some kind of urgent question that she hadn't even known she was asking. Reluctantly, she lifted her head from Sebastian's shoulder, and they looked at each other.

Then, moving with deliberation, he cupped the back of her neck, drew her forward and kissed her. When his firm, mobile lips met hers, she felt another much-needed answer. Her lips parted and he dove into her mouth deeply with his tongue, stunning her with the swiftness of his invasion.

Her world whirled in a kaleidoscopic tilt. She hadn't expected the kiss. She was still amazed that he had confided in her, and that they had embraced.

She hadn't expected this.

His mouth was wet, hard and demanding. Still kissing her, he pushed her back and back, and she complied until she came in contact with the wall. His body covered hers. He took her wrists, pinned her arms over her head and shoved one muscled, jeans-clad leg between hers. His movements were so aggressive, so surprising, a shaken moan broke out of her. Dear God, he had an erection. The hard length of it pressed against her hip.

He lit her world on fire. Everything burned with incandescent light.

She wanted to touch his hair to find out if it was as soft as it looked. She wanted to touch him. Her fingers opened and closed in fists. The hard shackles of his hands prevented her from touching him the way she needed to. All she could do was squeeze his leg between hers, arch against his body and kiss him back, so she did, while her heart took off on a manic gallop, running as fast as it could straight toward him.

His breath came and went rapidly, his wide chest working like a bellows. He drew back and stared at her, his strange, golden-amber-and-black gaze fierce. Along with the muscles of his lean body, the lines of his face had sharpened.

The realization crept in that she stared at an entirely dangerous man, and she had no idea what he would do next.

She also had no idea what *she* would do next.

"You could always just lock the door," she whispered. Goodness, the things that fell out of her mouth on this trip.

His face blazed. Looking utterly barbaric, he ground his hips against hers. It tore a ragged cry out of her, because she had *never* felt like this before, never. Not with any of her dates or former lovers. Normally she was a calm, considered person, a bit of a nerd if she were to be quite honest, but now a strange, crazed creature had taken over her body.

"Yo!" Bailey pounded on the door again. "The crew's starting to arrive."

He bared his teeth. He looked utterly savage. "I said I'm on my way!"

"Take your time," said Bailey. The other woman sounded extremely cheerful. "Just letting you know."

He hissed in the direction of the door. "Go the fuck away."

Olivia had focused her attention on the rapid pulse beating at the base of his strong jaw. She muttered, "Would you mind if I bit you?"

Wait, who just said that?

He released one of her wrists to yank his fingers violently through his speckled hair. "*God. Damn. Yes.* I mean no, I don't mind. *Yes*, you should bite me. As many times as you want." He thrust a stiffened finger under her nose. "We're going to continue this very soon. Got that, Olivia?"

She nodded drunkenly, staring at the finger. He kissed her again, swiftly and hard, and then with a growl he shoved away from her and the wall and strode out of the cabin.

Left to her own devices, her legs wouldn't support her. She slid into a shaking heap. Astonished euphoria sang a chorus and tap-danced in her veins.

Julian had been right. This had, indeed, turned into an interesting evening.

Fucking fuckers.

She clapped both hands over her face and burst out laughing. It sounded hysterical even to her own ears.

Slowly sanity set in, along with a clash of conflicting emotions that ricocheted like brightly colored billiard balls around in her head. She shoved to her feet and located Sebastian's bathroom. By general standards it was miniscule, just a small basin, toilet and a shower, but it was polished clean and it had the huge advantage of being private.

Or so she thought.

As she splashed cold water on her face, Phaedra solidified beside her. The Djinn announced, "I am ready for small talk now."

Olivia jerked upright and swiped at her dripping chin with the back of one hand. "*What*? No!"

Phaedra gave her an exasperated look and began to dematerialize.

"Phaedra, I'm sorry. Hold on a minute." As the Djinn paused, her form half-insubstantial, Olivia patted her face dry with Sebastian's hand towel. The cloth smelled freshly laundered. She folded it neatly on the rail and turned to Phaedra. "I'm rattled and preoccupied, and you startled me. I really didn't mean to cut you off like that. I wanted to thank you, not only for what you did earlier outside, but for agreeing to surround Sebastian's room with a barrier while Julian was on the ship."

Phaedra considered her with narrowed eyes. "I didn't do it for you. I did it for Khalil, and, in some measure, for Grace."

She took a steadying breath, and reached for patience and calm. "Nevertheless," she said quietly. "You helped me quite a bit this evening, and I am grateful. I know that you are not supposed to bargain for favors on this trip, but I'm offering one to you anyway. And if you ever need a friend, I hope you might consider me."

"I don't need friends," said Phaedra.

Unsurprised, she nodded. "If you ever change your mind, just let me know."

"Why did you kiss him?" Phaedra asked abruptly.

Well, that was like a dash of cold water in the face. She threw her hands up in the air. "I can't believe you were watching us!"

The Djinn twitched her shoulders in a shrug. "Of course, I was watching. What else would I be doing? This trip is boring."

Olivia's mouth dropped open. "You have got to be kidd—"

But Phaedra dissipated before she could finish the sentence.

As Olivia made her way to the cabin she shared with Dendera, voices echoed along the corridors. From the sound of things, everyone had returned successfully.

Exhaustion had replaced the euphoria, and she took advantage of the privacy to get ready for bed quickly. She was just slipping into her bunk when Dendera arrived.

"What a lot of fuss over nothing," Dendera said. The other symbologist looked as tired as Olivia felt. "At least we will be crossing over a few hours later in the morning."

"Thank God," she said.

Dendera didn't appear to welcome chitchat, and Olivia certainly wasn't in the mood. Pulling the covers up to her chin, she curled on her side. Immediately she was immersed in the memory of Sebastian's body moving over hers and the sensation of his tongue in her mouth. Warmth filled her body, and it was both hungry and languid.

She thought she would never fall asleep, but then, suddenly, she did.

Much too early, Derrick, the Elven male on the security crew who was crossing over, walked through the corridors and knocked on doors, waking everybody up. Breakfast was a quick, simple affair of hot coffee, Danish pastries and cranky people, several of whom appeared to be hung over.

Sebastian remained absent. Olivia's excited, nervous anticipation dimmed into a rather queasy feeling. Surely she must have imagined that raw, wide-open highway they had raced along together.

She escaped the breakfast table and took her coffee up to the deck where cold, bright sunshine pierced the air. Contemplating an affair with one's immediate supervisor was a recipe for disaster, anyway. If this job had been a permanent position, she would never even consider the possibility.

Time sped up in a flurry of activity as the crossover team donned their wetsuits. Everyone's mood improved drastically and a ragged cheer went up when the yacht pulled away from the dock. As people moved up to the deck, Sebastian appeared.

He wore his sunglasses again. His wetsuit molded the trim, powerful lines of his compact body, and a fitful wind ruffled his white-and-sable-flecked hair as he stepped light as a dancer between team members until he stood in front of Olivia.

Her hands had started to shake as he approached. She pushed her fists against her upper thighs as he looked down at her, his hard expression intent.

Then she noticed the taut lines bracketing the corners of his mouth. She asked very quietly, "Is everything all right?"

He replied in the same low voice, "Just another headache. I missed you last night."

Her breath turned choppy. She grew aware that a few of the others had turned to look at them. Bailey watched them, arms crossed and face expressionless. Steve stared too, and the distaste on his thin face was anything but expressionless.

Suddenly she didn't care. The tension between her and Sebastian's bodies vibrated like a strong, golden wire, urging her closer. Licking her lips, she whispered, "I missed you too."

He bent his head toward her, slowly, and realization sank in. He was giving her time to find some way to stop him or turn him away. It would be entirely her choice whether or not they let their budding connection become public.

But she could not imagine turning away from him in that moment.

Insane though it sounded, she could not imagine ever turning away from him.

Whoa, Nelly. Don't panic, it was just a thought. Of course they hardly knew each other, and falling in love that fast with a (near) total stranger was inconceivable, and…

Blah blah blah…

She let the supposedly calm, logical part of her mind babble away. In the meantime, she had more important things to do. Stepping forward, she raised her face and met his kiss halfway.

His firm lips settled over hers. Compared to the crazed escalation from the previous night, this kiss was positively tame, just nestling their lips together in a gesture that was more affectionate than anything else. He rested his hands on her hips, and she covered them with her own. The most intimate thing about it all was that it was so public.

Except that his hot, male Power wrapped around her, invisible and possessive, and the fire that he had started in her last night flared up again, hectic and out of control.

She managed not to reach out and clutch him to her in a totally inappropriate embrace, but her body shook with the effort. He held back too, but standing so close to him, she could feel the tension vibrating off his taut body. His fingers dug into the soft flesh of her hips. She knew he would leave marks on her pale skin. She didn't mind. She wanted to egg him on.

So the crazed creature that had taken over her body was still in residence, alive and well. She drew back, mouth trembling.

His well-formed lips pulled into the sexiest smile she had ever seen, and the laugh lines bracketing his mouth deepened.

In the meantime, silence had descended on deck. She glanced around cautiously. Dendera looked shocked, and almost everyone got very busy, all except for Bailey, who gave her a thumbs up and a grin.

And Steve, who stared at her with a cold, unfriendly gaze.

Chapter Seven

After all their preparation, and despite Sebastian's concerns about the inexperienced symbologists, the crossover went without a hitch. Phaedra sank into the ocean with them and shortly afterward the Djinn's physical form dissipated as she settled at the passageway's entrance.

Bailey swam along the passageway first, hauling two containers that had been carefully weighted so that they floated a few feet above the sea floor. She cast magical light spells as she went. The balls of light flared and then slowly faded, giving everybody that followed plenty of illumination for their journey.

Behind her mask, Olivia's expression was full of wonder as they swam along the passageway. Sebastian stayed close beside her protectively, but she made an excellent crossing. They both hauled containers. She transported empty ones designed for the library collection, and he pulled food supplies and packs.

Land magic swirled around them, and partway through the trip the seabed changed. They couldn't rise to the surface with the containers, so they swam until the water grew shallow enough that they could stand. Then they pushed back their masks and stared at the land in front of them.

A sandy beach lay directly ahead of them just yards away. A bluff rose from the beach, with a path zigzagging up the side. The heavy gold sunlight of late afternoon drenched the scene. A stone fence ran along the top of the bluff, and beyond that, a partially visible manor house sprawled.

Underneath the constant murmur of the surf and the sound of wind, a certain kind of silence lay over the scene, a complete lack of traffic or any other man-made sounds. A bird of some kind called in the distance, warbling a sharp warning of their arrival.

They knew from information that Carling had given them that the island was kidney-shaped and four miles long. Behind the house was an extensive vegetable garden and a path that led to a cottage that held her library.

At the other end of the island, an ancient forest of redwoods towered to the sky. The forest was where the shy, winged creatures lived, and as Carling had said when she had briefed Sebastian, there was no reason for any of their group to go to that part of the island. They would only frighten the creatures that lived among the redwoods, and their job lay elsewhere.

Two by two, the rest of the crew rose to the surface of the water to stand alongside him and Olivia and stare at the scene.

"All right," said Sebastian after a minute. "Checking out the library is going to have to wait until morning.

We've got a lot of work to do. We have to haul ass if we're going to get set up before dark."

"You heard the man," said Bailey. She had already dragged her containers to shore and stood knee deep in the foamy swirl of water with her legs braced apart and her wetsuit partially unzipped. "Hop to it. Just remember—at the end of today's work, we get to help ourselves to Carling's wine cellar." She grinned at Sebastian. "Hell, I would have taken the job for that reason alone."

"It *is* an incentive," he said. He unzipped a waterproof pouch, pulled out his sunglasses and slipped them on before any of the others could get a chance to look at his eyes.

The next several hours were filled with nonstop physical labor. Sebastian sent Tony and Derrick into the manor house first to check it out, as the rest of them hauled containers and supplies up the bluff path.

The two men came out again quickly enough. After being uninhabited for so long, the house was dusty and occupied with mice, and a few windows had broken, probably from high winds.

But there was plenty of wood stacked in the large kitchen and in woodpiles out the back, and there were fireplaces in every room, a large stockpile of beeswax candles, and also plenty of linens and blankets stored in cedar chests. All of the chimneys were sound, except for one that had some kind of blockage—probably a nest of some kind. The water pumps in the kitchen and washroom worked.

There was also a wide variety of food in sealed jars and cans that could supplement their food supplies. They had come prepared for rough conditions, but in actuality they would be staying in a great deal of comfort. Compared to some of the places Sebastian had camped in for some jobs, this would be like a stay at the Hilton.

The security team traveled back to the yacht to bring over the last of the supplies and more empty containers for the library. Carling's library filled a cottage, and it would take several more trips to bring all of the containers over, but that was a task that could happen over time.

After bringing everything up the bluff except for their oxygen tanks, which they left wrapped in tarps at the base of the path, they took turns in the large washroom to change out of their wetsuits and leave them hanging to dry. Then they hauled wood and laid fires in fireplaces, beat mattresses and made beds, and nailed wooden planks across the broken windows.

The house was big. While they would have to take turns heating water and using the large washroom behind the kitchen, they could each have their own bedroom. The food supplies were taken to the kitchen, and the empty library containers were stacked in the great hall. As the light of day faded, they filled and lit glass and metal lanterns, and Derrick and Steve even swept the main halls clear of debris.

Finally, Bailey disappeared into the wine cellar while Dendera and Tony scrubbed the large kitchen table with hot water and soap. Olivia and Derrick laid out their supper—cheese and crackers, fresh fruit, and rotisserie chicken that had been packed in ice for the trip. Raiding the pantry, they added olives, nuts and dried fruits, and finally the tired crew members gathered at the table.

Sebastian said, "Dendera, Steve and Olivia, your jobs are in the library, so this doesn't apply do you, but Bailey, Tony, Derrick and I will take watches at night. Tomorrow we'll tour the island, or at least the part of the island not covered by the redwoods. Tony and Derrick, you'll take the watch tonight."

His people knew the drill, and they nodded, unsurprised.

Steve looked up as he stacked food on his plate and said, "Are you sure that's necessary? There's nobody here but us."

"That's not quite correct," said Sebastian. "The only thing we know for sure is that the crossover passageway has not been guarded 24/7 since Carling left. We'll do as Carling ordered and nobody will go into the forest. But we will maintain watches, just to be safe."

Bailey reappeared with several dusty bottles in her arms, eyes wide with glee. As everyone in the kitchen turned to look at her, she said, "Hey, the lady wants her library, not her wine. Oh my God, look at this vintage."

Sebastian chose not to sit at the table with the others. He leaned back against the counter, taking a break for the first time since diving off the yacht earlier that day. His headache had faded several hours ago. Now he was clearheaded and edgy. Restlessness ran underneath his skin.

Earlier he had taken a lap around the house to study the immediate terrain. The flat ocean horizon gave the illusion that this small nugget of Other land was vast and limitless, when in reality, according to Carling, when one sailed away from the island, one would somehow end up coming right back. The vegetable garden at the back of the house had long since turned into an overgrown jungle of weeds. He had walked the path to the cottage where the library was housed, then back again, while subtle whispers of magic skittered along the edges of his mind like furtive mice.

He could still feel those magic whispers, a sensation like the brush of cobwebs against his skin, although the greater distance from the cottage weakened them. Something in the library was restless too.

As Bailey wiped off the wine bottles and uncorked them, he studied each individual. The other three members of his security team, Bailey, Derrick and Tony, were having a good time. They joked with each other and made friendly overtures to Dendera, Steve and Olivia. Olivia laughed at his crew's jokes and responded in kind. Dendera was the most reserved of the group, but she smiled at the others and at him.

Steve was different. He was a predator Wyr and a symbologist, a combination of characteristics that interested Sebastian. He smelled like some kind of canine, perhaps a coyote. Sebastian had already noted that Steve went out of his way to avoid him.

He had also noticed Steve's friendly attitude toward Olivia on the flight, but since then the other Wyr's attitude had done a one-eighty. After Sebastian had marked his claim on Olivia back on the deck of the yacht, Steve refused to look at Olivia, and he went out of his way to avoid her too.

Was the other man jealous? Sebastian smiled coldly. Steve didn't have a chance with Olivia, so he could just dream on.

Sebastian's restlessness ratcheted higher. He should eat, but he didn't want to.

What he *wanted* had not left his mind all day.

He watched Olivia steadily, his patience eroding fast. She wore a soft blue cable knit sweater and jeans, and it was the sexiest outfit he had ever seen. Her breasts and hips rounded gently from a narrow waist, and her lovely, intelligent gray eyes lit with laughter as she responded to something that Bailey said.

Like Steve, she didn't look at Sebastian either. Unlike Steve, he knew very well why she avoided his gaze. Sensual awareness shimmered in the air between them. Hell, it all but threw confetti and lit fireworks.

Flashes of what he had done to her, of what she had said to him, played in his mind.

Would you mind if I bit you?

The question had floored him. It was not just that she had been able to ask it—it was that she asked so politely. The very act had spoken volumes.

It said that she hadn't ever had a lover drive her to bite and scratch. When you reached that level of passion, you didn't pause to politely ask permission. At that point, permission would have already been given and received.

I will take you to that place, he thought. Where no man has ever taken you before.

He said to her telepathically, *Your room or mine?*

She had just taken a sip of wine, and she choked and coughed while Bailey pounded her on the back. Color flushed Olivia's face, and her gaze turned brilliant and sparkling. When she replied, even her mental voice sounded strangled. *I don't care. Either. Both?*

Laughter flashed through the heat building up in his veins. It was another surprise.

We'll start with yours, he said. Then, because he could not stay in that room full of people and pretend to be civilized, he stalked out of the kitchen.

He knew which room she had chosen. He had watched earlier as she had looked outside and carefully marked the path of the sun. Then she had picked the bedroom that would fill with early morning light. As she had disappeared inside with her pack, he claimed the room adjacent to hers. Now he slipped into her room silently, removed his sunglasses and set them on a nearby table.

He stood at the window in the darkened room and looked up at the bright spray of stars in the night sky.

The moon called to him. It always called to him.

Come dance with me, it said. Take wing and fly wild into the night.

And he always had, before now.

This time, he said to the moon, I cannot fly with you this night, for I have another with whom I will dance, and she is even lovelier than you.

And the knowledge of that was both bitter and sweet, as he let go of one thing to reach for the other.

A few minutes later, he heard her footsteps in the hall. He already knew what her footsteps sounded like, quick and light on the hardwood floor. He would recognize her step anywhere.

He turned from the window without a backward glance as she slipped through the door, and with the acute senses of a predator, he knew that she was trembling. He closed his eyes and drew in everything about her.

She gave him a wealth of sensations. Her unique feminine scent drifted delicately through the air, filled with complexity and desire. The bare vulnerability of her ragged breathing played a solo for an audience of one.

His heart, which had grown so cramped with stress, fear and anger over the last several months, expanded, and he thought, It would not be so terrible to be blind like this.

And for that one moment alone, no matter what else happened between them or how badly this might end, he would be forever grateful to her.

Then he opened his eyes again and looked his fill of her. The barest hint of moonlight in the room was enough for his still sharp vision. It followed the curve of her cheek, and gleamed in her shadowed gaze. As he watched her lick her lips, his erection grew full, hot and tight.

As she hesitated, he remembered she had a human's senses, and he said quietly, "I'm here."

There, that catch in her breath. He drank it down as if it were the finest wine.

Then suddenly he was angry. He was so angry, he was filled with rage. Rage at his dead enemy, rage at himself. He didn't want this. He needed to be selfish right now, goddamn it, yet he could not exorcise regret.

"Where are your friends, and why aren't they looking out for you?" he snapped. He stalked toward her. "What are you doing here with me? Don't you know you have no *business* being with a man under a curse? How foolish can you get?"

The dark room reverberated with the lash of his anger. She stood quite still. He grabbed her by the shoulders, and only then did she move.

She lunged forward, knocking clumsily into his chest as she threw her arms around his neck and clenched him tight. "It's okay," she said. She sounded quiet and strong, and very sure of herself. "I'm okay. You are going to be okay."

Astonished, he let her hold him. "You don't know that."

She stroked his hair. "I know that I didn't give you permission to look out for me," she said. "I can and will look out for myself, and I will be okay because I say so."

He moved his hands compulsively down her back. She was exquisitely shaped, nature's violin, playing that invisible, ineffable thing that was her spirit. He did not know that he could feel such anguish at her beauty, or such...exultation.

"You're pulling me out of my body," he muttered.

"Shhh," she whispered. She cupped the back of his head and drew him down to her, and when she kissed him, their lips nestled together again just as they had that morning. He experienced a weird, sensual sort of synesthesia. Their kiss was like a hug, and as he slipped his hands underneath her sweater, the touch of his fingers was like a kiss on her warm skin.

Their bodies shifting together made a delicate, intimate sound. He drew her sweater up, and she helped him by raising her arms over her head. As he reached for her again, he discovered that her soft, round breasts were already bared for his touch. He cupped them, exploring their weight and shape. The velvet jut of her nipples pushed into his palms.

When he flicked the sensitive, delicate flesh with his thumbs, she let her head fall back as she made a muffled sound, gripped at his wrists and shuddered.

The line of her slender, exposed throat cut him loose. Control skidded away, and he turned into an animal. She cried out as he grabbed her by the waist, lifted and threw her onto the nearby bed. Then he sprang. He was on her so fast her body didn't have time to bounce on the mattress. With rough, jerky movements he undid the fastening of her jeans and yanked them down her hips.

While he worked on undressing her, she took hold of his T-shirt and pulled, her hands shaking with urgency.

He barely noticed until it restricted the movements of his arms. Then he had to pause, growling, to yank his shirt over his head. As he did so, she sat up and ran her palms down the extended length of his muscled torso to the fastening of his jeans. Her trembling fingers fumbled at the button.

He put his hands over hers and squeezed. "I've got it," he muttered.

"Hurry."

That single word, said in such an agonized whisper, sent a line of fire down his spine.

He rolled away from her and tore off his clothes. When he reached for her again, he found that she had finished kicking her jeans and panties off and was naked too.

He fell on her ravenously. The sense of her naked, curvaceous body against his sent a wave of heat over his skin. He yanked her thighs apart and felt between her legs. Under a soft tangle of short hair, her private flesh felt plump and swollen, slick with wetness, and his erection tightened until it was an actual pain. She smelled and felt like an invitation. He came down on her and positioned his cock at her drenched, fluted entrance.

Vaguely, in the back of his mind, he knew this wasn't the way to go about doing things. He hissed, "Foreplay."

Way to class it up, dickhead.

She gasped, "Next time."

She pulled at his shoulders and arched her pelvis up. He threw back his head and thrust into her. Her slick passage gripped him tighter than a fist. He shook his head, growling as he trembled all over, trying to give her time to adjust to his abrupt invasion.

But then she squeezed him with her inner muscles and undulated her sexy body so that he slid out partway and then back in, and he descended completely into madness.

He grabbed her by the hair and rutted on her. She cried out and clawed at his back, trying to draw him in deeper as she lifted herself for every thrust.

"Are you going to bite me or not?" he snarled.

She bared her teeth at him. She looked as crazed as he felt. Then she twisted at her torso and sank her teeth into his biceps. She bit him so hard he felt her little teeth break the skin.

Delight suffused him, along with a fierce, feral satisfaction. Still fucking her, he slid an arm underneath her shoulders to lift her up. Then he bit her too, sinking his teeth into the hollow where her neck met her shoulder. He pumped in, and in, and she clenched her arms and legs around him as her body jerked and shuddered, and he felt her climax in a ripple of intense contractions.

She brought him along with her. Bending his head to the pillow beside her head, his own climax spewed out of him convulsively. As she shivered and groaned, it pulled more of him, wave upon wave of frenzied pleasure.

Gradually they stilled, their bodies slick with sweat. Her breathing sounded in his ear, ragged gasps like shallow sobs. As he buried his face against her, she hooked an arm around his neck to hold him loosely.

She had linked her ankles together at the small of his back. He lifted his head and looked down at her. She gave him a vulnerable, luminous smile. Her expression was utterly gorgeous. When she started to open her legs to let him go, he gripped her thigh.

Her breath hitched.

He whispered against her lips, “I’m not done yet.”

Chapter Eight

He broke her wide open, until something raw and trembling and utterly new crawled out of her old, outdated skin, and it was more fierce and possessive than she had ever been before.

She watched out her window as predawn gradually lightened her bedroom. Then she curled on her side facing Sebastian. He slept stretched out on his stomach, his head half buried by pillows. Even though the room was chilly, he had pushed the blankets down to his hips.

Her gaze followed the peaks and hollows of his wide shoulders and biceps and down his muscled back. His tanned skin bore the marks she had made on him, long scratches on his back and the reddened bite mark on his arm, already fading.

She lifted the covers to look at herself. He had marked her too. Bruises dotted her hips and thighs, and the bite he had given her, at the juncture of her neck, felt tender and sensitive to the touch. But she was only human, and the marks on her body would not be as quick to fade.

She slipped a hand between her legs. She felt throbbing and sore below too. He had spent himself on her again and again, and he had wrung more climaxes out of her than she had ever thought possible. And she was fiercely glad for all of it.

She also knew what that could mean. It was possible—just barely possible—that he might be beginning to mate with her. It was too soon to know, of course. It was too soon for everything. Only time could tell if he would mate with her, or if he would pull away, or if this complete, full-blown obsession she had developed for him would turn out to be love.

But she thought, at least in her case, that it was the beginnings of falling in love. She really thought it was. He was fine and fierce, complicated and quite extraordinary, and the strength of emotion and vulnerability he had shown to her surpassed anything she had ever experienced from anyone else. He engaged all of her senses, emotions and intellect in a perfect trifecta.

Yes, I think I could grow to love you, she thought, as she looked at the back of his tousled head. I think I could grow to love you so much, I would do anything, give up anything, for you. So don't back away from us. Give us time.

Of course she didn't say any of that aloud. A sensible, sane person wouldn't dream of saying any of that after spending just one single night with someone, however extraordinary that night had been.

So the new, trembling, fierce thing inside of her would keep silent for now, and watch, and pretend to be sensible and sane.

She leaned forward and pressed a kiss to his bare shoulder. He stirred and rolled over, his tough face eased from sleep, and he gathered her into his arms. She went gladly, curling her tired, sore body to his. He cupped the back of her head, fitting her to his shoulder, and pressed a kiss to her forehead. She stroked her flattened hand along his lean chest, which was bare of hair.

Then she drifted with him, lightly along the edge of sleep, until the smell of brewed coffee wafted up from the kitchen, and the morning sunlight shone full and bright.

Breakfast was another quick, simple affair of coffee, leftover chicken, cheese and crackers, and fruit. After carefully inspecting the sealed jars in the huge pantry, Derrick declared that he might have fresh-baked bread for them later in the day.

Derrick, Tony and Bailey all made a point of smiling at Olivia and doing a dozen little things that said they were welcoming her into the fold. She was warmed by it, not only for her sake, but also for Sebastian's. They cared about him, and that spoke volumes for the quality of his character and leadership.

Dendera's attitude remained the same, reserved but not unfriendly, and Steve kept himself aloof, which, as far as she was concerned, was just as well. If he tried to tell her any more negative gossip she might haul off and hit him.

Once they finished the morning meal, Derrick and Tony took care of cleaning up. The three symbologists gathered the first batch of hermetically sealed containers and headed down the path to the cottage. Sebastian and Bailey insisted on accompanying them.

"There's no need for you to do that," Dendera told them.

"There's every need," said Sebastian. In full sunlight, he looked suntanned and vital, his personality as forceful as ever. As always, he wore his sunglasses, but now Olivia could read the subtleties of his expression behind the barrier as he looked at her and gave her a slight smile. "Your safety is my responsibility, and I reserve the right to yank all of you out of there if things get out of control. Carling said to stay sharp and be careful, and that's exactly what we're going to do."

Olivia smiled back at him. Then, as she turned away, she caught sight of Steve. He was staring at Sebastian with an expression of such naked hostility it caused her to stop in her tracks.

What on *earth*?

But in the next instant the expression was gone, leaving her to wonder if she had imagined the whole thing as Steve turned to follow Dendera down the path.

Finally, after months of hard work and planning, they approached their destination. The area around the cottage was overgrown with weeds. The building itself looked humble and ordinary, but tendrils of uncontained magic ghosted through the air.

Dendera took the lead and opened the cottage door. There was a large workroom just inside. It hadn't been tidied after its last use.

Dendera said, "We'll stack the containers in here until we fill them."

Bailey and Sebastian remained wary, their eyes sharp. Olivia set the two containers she carried alongside the others. She straightened to assess the erratic magic calmly. She met Dendera's gaze. "We'll have to follow each thread back to its source."

The other woman nodded. "Once we get those works contained, we'll be able to pack up the rest of the collection at our leisure." She took a deep breath. "For now it's probably safest if we work in pairs."

Olivia couldn't help it. She looked at Sebastian, who said immediately, "I'm your partner."

Perhaps it was silly to feel such happiness at his words. Certainly it was silly to read too much into it. Despite scolding herself to be sensible, she did both.

Dendera said, "Steve, you and I will pair up today."

"Right," said Bailey, as she bounced on the balls of her feet and looked around. Her long, elegantly pointed ears peeked through the curls of her short, tousled hair. "And I'll...just...keep an eye on this room, shall I?"

"The only way to start doing this is to pick a magical thread and follow it," said Olivia. She picked one of the strongest, most erratic magical threads and began to trace it to its source.

It led her down a hall, past rooms with filled bookcases. Sebastian followed on her heels. He stayed so close that she could sense his body heat on her bare arm. With an effort she had to turn her attention away from his presence and focus on the task at hand.

She followed the magical thread to a leather-bound book in a corner bookshelf.

"There you are," she whispered as she squatted in front of it. With a careful, practiced eye, she mentally translated the archaic title on the faded leather spine. *Instructions on Angelic Visitations and Demonic Summoning.* "This is a medieval grimoire, a very old book of spells. The oldest books are always the most unruly."

Sebastian asked in her ear, "What are you going to do about it?"

She wagged a finger gently in the air without looking at him. "I'm going to do my job, and you are not going to distract me. Either that or Bailey can come help me."

"Bailey's not going to help you," he growled. "I am."

She bit back a smile. "Then be quiet."

In the vast variety of magical books and treatises that Olivia had encountered throughout her professional life, they all had one thing in common—books wanted to be opened. The key to handling an unruly magical book was to make sure one's own Power was quiescent, so that it didn't trigger some kind of backlash or attack.

Carefully she extended one hand, letting the magical energy of the grimoire adjust to her nearing presence. When she finally laid her fingers on the leather cover, it didn't react.

She pulled it off the shelf, and it came smoothly, even eagerly. As she held it in one hand, she said, "*Claudo.*" At the same time she uttered the single word spell, she sketched the symbol for "close" over the front cover.

Despite its unruliness, it was still a book. The magic it contained snapped shut.

She looked over her shoulder and smiled at Sebastian's fascinated expression. "One down. Many more to go."

They worked through the morning. By lunchtime the air in the cottage was beginning to feel much more settled. After eating, Sebastian and Bailey returned to the library with the symbologists, but by midafternoon it became clear that their assistance was no longer needed, so they took off to fish for their supper. Sebastian gave her a quick, hard kiss before he left.

The symbologists continued to work until early evening and the shadows in the cottage grew dark. Dendera told Olivia and Steve, "We will stop now. We've done a good first day's work."

Steve looked up from the open container where he was carefully packing a five-volume set. "I'll keep working."

Dendera shook her head, her round features softening with a smile. "I know how hard it is to pull yourself away. This library is fascinating, and I could keep working through the night as well. But I don't want anybody to work on the collection on their own. We'll leave together."

"There's so much to do, and I'm not tired," he argued. He waved a hand in the direction of the rooms full of books. "You can sense for yourself that we've contained the most unruly magics."

"I'm sorry, but I'm just not willing to take that chance," said Dendera. "We've got plenty of time, and it will all be waiting for us in the morning."

Olivia watched with interest as Steve's expression tightened with frustration. He did not like being told no. But all he said was, "If you think that's best."

"I do."

He shrugged. "When do you think we'll start work on the papyri collection?"

"We should be ready to tackle that section in a few days," Dendera said. "Let's go eat supper."

The next several days fell into a pattern that was pure bliss for Olivia. The mild days were full of seemingly endless sunshine, and the nights turned chilly enough to call for fires, blankets and hot tea.

She immersed herself in all of her passions. By day, she handled rare and unique books. In the evening they ate freshly caught fish, grilled with wild onions and garlic, and sweet dates and almonds drizzled with honey, and they drank rare wine.

At night she explored every manner of sensual pleasure with Sebastian whenever he was free. He did not sleep alone. Either he took his turn at keeping watch, or he stayed with her. He drove her to exhaustion, and when she couldn't take any more, they piled blankets on the floor in front of the fire and he would painstakingly massage her sore, tired body with the essential oils that he had found in one of the rooms.

In the mornings they would talk drowsily, nesting in the warm bed until it was time to get up for the day.

He told her of his life in Jamaica, and as he talked, he never stopped touching her. Stroking her thigh. Running his fingers through her short hair. Following the curve of her breast with a finger. The constant contact drenched her in pleasure.

She lay draped across him bonelessly as she listened, and it didn't matter what he told her. He could have been talking about accounting or mathematic algorithms, and she would have loved it. The fact that he actually opened up to her made it even more special.

"How did you and Bailey meet?" she asked.

"We grew up together in New Orleans." She could hear the smile in his voice. "She's more than a friend. She's like my little sister."

"I think you guys have a wonderful relationship." Olivia smiled too. She loved to watch them bicker.

"Looking back," he said, "I can't believe we made a go of the company. We did almost everything wrong. At least we learned from our mistakes."

She walked her fingers up his chest as she said, "And you had to have done more things right than not, because you *did* make a go of it."

"Eventually." He captured her hand and lifted it to kiss her fingers.

Her mind flashed, without her consent, back to Steve's negative gossip. "Why Jamaica?" she asked. "Why not the Wyr demesne in New York?"

"I respect what Dragos has done for the Wyr," he said. "I can even see that there is a necessary place for it in the world, but his brand of nationalism bothers me. I prefer a more inclusive approach to life. We hire anybody based on their talents and resources as an individual, regardless of whether or not they are Wyr or some other Elder Race, or if they are human."

"Like Tony?"

"Yes, exactly. Tony's human, but he's a great fighter, he has a little bit of magic, and while he might not be a doctor, he is a damn fine field medic. All of that makes him a strong, versatile member of any crew." He shrugged, his shoulders shifting fluidly underneath her stroking fingers. "And of course we could have done all of that in New York too. But that's where the answer to your other question comes in. Sun, warmth, sandy beaches, endless beautiful water. Hell, we based the company in Jamaica just because we could."

She grinned. "You must get a lot of applicants for job openings."

"Quite a few," he said dryly.

"How many people do you employ?"

"Almost a hundred. We're still technically a small company."

She blew out a soundless whistle. "It sounds like a big company to me. I had no idea."

He chuckled. "Sometimes having so many employees is almost like having that many children." Then he paused. "Don't tell any of them that I said that."

"I won't," she told him. "Probably." He bit her forefinger in retaliation, and she laughed. "And anyway, employees and children are nothing alike."

He sighed. "I'm sure you're right. At least none of my employees need to be diapered."

She chuckled, and he rolled her over, reversing their positions, so that she lay on her back and his head rested on her shoulder. Then, lazily, he played with her nipple, and even though they had made love through the night until she had fallen asleep out of sheer exhaustion, she felt arousal stir at his touch.

"How about you?" he asked. His voice had turned very quiet so that she almost couldn't hear him. "Have you ever considered having them? Children, I mean. Not employees."

She went still, turning her face into his hair as she listened to the nuances in his question. Then she whispered, "The right relationship never came along, and I never wanted to have children on my own. But if I found the right partner…"

Dare she say it?

She realized that he had gone as still as she had. That he seemed to be holding his breath. That gave her the courage to whisper, "With the right partner, I would adore having children."

Then he moved and sighed, and pressed a kiss against the side of her breast as he spread one hand over her flat abdomen. "I love children," he said simply. "And you would make a beautiful mother."

Luminous emotion filled her as she imagined him with his own children. He would make an incredible father, strong, protective, patient and loving. The image was so compelling, it made her chest ache. She covered his hand with hers and pressed her lips against his forehead.

They fell silent and lay like that for some time, until he stirred and said, “Tell me more about Louisville.”

It was hard to let go of the moment, but then she followed his cue and talked of her life and friends in Louisville, and Brutus her cat, who was currently staying at her parents’ house.

Neither one of them broached the subject of how they would continue seeing each other when they left the island, although they came close to it several times. She wanted to talk about it, but each day she fell further and further in love with him, and she grew more and more afraid of what might happen next.

She could leave her life and friends to live with him in Jamaica, and she could build a new life there that would make her very happy. But what she couldn’t do was live Sebastian’s life of constant adventure.

She knew she could never ask him to settle down and hope that he could change that completely. Sooner or later, even if he did grow to love her too—even if he did mate with her—she was afraid that he would get tired of being in one place and end up feeling trapped. And that would be intolerable for the both of them.

Still, despite her growing trepidation for what the future might hold, she couldn't turn him away when he came to her room. He drew her too powerfully.

During the daytime hours, the symbologists methodically worked from section to section and room to room in the library, handling works from all nationalities and races—French, medieval, Chinese, Hungarian, early American, and Greek and Roman auguries. Light and Dark Fae works, Elven, Nightkind and Demonkind. Books on Wyr magic, Other lands and the Elder gods, and books upon books on Vampyrism.

Finally one morning they reached the Egyptian section, which contained the papyri collection, and Steve's attention grew sharper and more focused.

Olivia wasn't the only one who noticed. Dendera asked him, "Have you studied Egyptology or Egyptian magic?"

"My employer has," Steve replied. "He's talked quite a bit about it, and it's piqued my interest."

"Don't you work for Edinburgh University's Magical Depository?" Dendera asked.

"Currently I do," he said. "I'm talking about another employer."

Did that sound odd?

As she locked the lid of one container into place, Olivia frowned, drawn in spite of herself into the conversation. "Do you mean a former employer?"

Steve didn't reply, and her frown deepened.

She had grown used to Steve being a bit of a dick, but this was something entirely different. To get hired for this job, he had to have gone through the same thorough background check as everyone else, but she couldn't help but wonder what Sebastian would make of Steve's behavior.

She glanced at the angle of sunshine streaming in through the nearby window. It was only midmorning. She wouldn't see Sebastian until lunch, still a few hours away, but she was definitely going to tell him about the conversation.

As they talked, they had started work on the most ancient section of the papyri collection. Dendera knelt in a corner and carefully drew out a thick scroll from the cubicle where it had been stored.

"Carling's instructions are very specific," she breathed. "We handle these as little as possible, and transfer them directly to the container. Look at this one. The original wax seal is unbroken. It has survived all these centuries."

Steve knelt beside Dendera and leaned forward. Olivia left the container she had just closed to walk over. The papyrus scroll was tied with what looked like a strip of leather, and the wax seal was unusually large and thick. The wax had darkened from what had probably been originally a golden brown. Now, either magic or time, or both, had turned it almost black. A sigil had been inscribed into the wax while it was still warm and soft.

"What is that mark?" Olivia asked. After all of this time, she could still feel the strong ward that lay imprinted in the wax. "What does it say?"

"*Khewew*," Dendera whispered. "'It has evil.'"

"Well, hot fucking damn," said Steve as he reached into the back pocket of his jeans. "It's about time."

His words were so strange that both women stared at him. He pulled something out of his pocket—a switch-blade. The blade flicked out, and, quicker than thought, he stabbed Dendera in the throat.

Dendera dropped the papyrus scroll and clutched at her throat, gagging as bright arterial blood spurted between her fingers.

Olivia's mind went into shock, but her body took over. She leaped to her feet and jumped away from Steve.

She wasn't fast enough. He was Wyr and so much faster than she. He leaped toward her and his knife flashed out.

One of the first things she had learned as a symbolo-gist was a series of defensive spells in case something went awry at work. She flung out her hand, fingers splayed. "*Avertere.*"

Avert.

The spell was meant to avert destructive magics, but thrown with enough force, it averted other things as well. It hit Steve squarely in the chest. As it knocked him into the wall, she whirled and ran.

The cottage wasn't large. She raced down the short hall, through the workroom. She flung the door open, even as she sensed Steve coming up behind her.

She wasn't going to make it. She spun to throw an-other avert spell at him, and he stabbed her in the chest. She felt the blade slip into her body, between her ribs.

Instinct told her the wound was very bad. She fell backward in a sprawl, blinking as Steve wiped his blade clean on the leg of her jeans, closed the switchblade and pocketed it again. Warm wetness spread across her T-shirt and spilled in a spreading puddle across the floor.

"I wanted to spare you ladies this," he said. "But Dendera wouldn't let me work on the library on my own. Every time I tried to sneak out at night, some damned person was standing guard, and they're all much better fighters than you two. Sorry about that, it's just how it all worked out."

He disappeared down the hall. A moment later, he returned, carrying the scroll. When he paused to study her with a narrow-eyed glance, she closed her eyes to slits, lay very still and pretended she was unconscious or dead.

She must have been convincing, because he turned back to his work. Through her eyelashes, she watched as he shifted a stack of filled containers until he reached the bottom one, which he opened.

The container held some of the most dangerous and expensive items in the library. She knew, because she had helped Steve pack it. He carefully tucked the scroll inside, locked the container and hefted it up, and walked out of the cottage.

Her hands and feet grew colder, and each breath became more difficult. Then she must have passed out, because she went blank for a formless time.

She came back to awareness with a start.

Sebastian.

Along with defensive spells, every symbologist also learned how to call for assistance. It was essential when one worked daily with Powerful and often unpredictable items.

The critical question, of course, was whether or not there would be anybody near enough to hear it.

The spell would be stronger if it was drawn in her own blood. Dipping her finger in the warm, sticky pool, she fought to pull her scattering Power together, and to punch all of her remaining strength into the symbol that she drew on the hardwood floor.

Help.

Chapter Nine

Sebastian was cursed and going blind, and he had never been happier. He was going to have to tell Olivia that he was mating with her, but he held back for now. They had known each other all of a week, and he didn't want to scare her away.

Mating, for Wyr, was a delicate, difficult business, especially when they mated with non-Wyr. Olivia could decide to end their relationship, but after a certain point of no return, Sebastian never would.

He thought he had not quite reached that place, but he would soon.

Each day he held off was a day they could both live in the present without dealing with pressure, concerns of the future or other implications. Each day gave her more opportunity to fall in love with him in return. She was steady and reliable, intelligent and caring, and each day he grew to trust her more and more. If she fell in love with him, she would never let him go. She was made for a lifetime of marriage.

He had so much to say to her, words upon words that piled up in his chest.

How tired he had become of everything in his life. How much he was looking forward to giving up the constant travel, and how he was looking forward to the adventure of learning what it meant to have a home life. To have a real home with someone who relished nesting, and who could teach him all the best ways to enjoy it. And how much he was looking forward to taking her traveling from time to time, and relearning how to love the experience of new things through her wonder and delight.

They could find an ideal balance between both lifestyles, living not one or the other, but a little bit of both. He knew it.

He knew it.

The conviction renewed his determination to find a way to break the curse. Everything he could possibly want was just within his grasp, and he refused to relinquish any of it.

He could live blind with her, if he had to. When they talked alone, she broached the subject constantly with kindness, pragmatism and optimism, until gradually she convinced him of it.

She had read articles about a blinded avian Wyr who took regular flights with her companion avian Wyr, her mate, who flew along with her. They coasted thermals together for hours. When it came time to end the flight, he would come up underneath his mate in midflight. Then she could grab hold of him and he would bring them both safely down to the ground.

"All we would need to do is find you a seeing-eye Wyr," Olivia said, her head on his chest. "Not that it will come to that."

He pressed his lips to her forehead and didn't reply, because they both knew if he was going to continue flying that it might.

In the meantime, when she was working, he flew every chance he could. The others didn't mind his absence. The security team's duties were light while the symbologists packed the library, and in any case, they cared about him enough to stay silent.

He relished the warmth of the sun on his wings as he circled around their end of the island. Often he closed his eyes as he rode thermals and imagined that other mated pair of avian Wyr.

He did so now, drifting through the air almost drowsily.

The job of packing would be finished in another week, then everybody would be busy transporting the containers across the passageway. By the time they were finished, reports from all his research teams would be waiting for him on the yacht.

If they had not found anything that could help him, he would consult with the Oracle right away. He did not expect that the teams would have found anything to contradict what Carling had already told him.

Tonight, he decided, he would ask Olivia if she would travel to Florida with him when he petitioned the Oracle.

Something flared against his magic sense from below, a hot, bright explosion from a Power that had become almost as familiar to him as his own.

Help.

His eyes snapped open. Olivia.

As quickly as the explosion had flared, it faded again.

He wheeled, folded his wings and hurtled down toward the cottage. On his dives he could reach speeds up to a hundred miles an hour. It didn't feel fast enough.

As he approached, he saw Bailey racing toward the cottage. Derrick followed close behind, and so did Tony. Just before he landed, he pulled up to coast a few feet above the ground. Shifting in midflight from an owl to a man at a dead run, he reached the cottage first.

The door was open. He lunged inside, and immediately had to skid to a stop. Olivia sprawled on the floor, her T-shirt soaked in ruby liquid. Stunned, he dropped to his knees beside her. *There was so much blood.* She lay in a pool of it. One of her arms lay stretched out, her hand cupped over a glyph of fading Power. She had drawn it in her own blood.

Panic seized him in razor sharp talons. He tore her T-shirt open as he roared, "*Derrick!*"

Bailey slammed through the doorway. "He's coming." She hitched momentarily as she took in the scene. "Oh fuck." Then she ricocheted off the wall to tear through the rest of the cottage.

Just underneath the lacy pink bra Sebastian had watched Olivia put on only a few hours ago, a thin, narrow puncture marred her creamy skin. It seeped a steady trickle of blood. Holy gods, that looked like a knife wound. His hands shook as he tore off his shirt and wadded the soft cotton material to apply pressure to it. He felt rather than heard a soft exhalation from her.

There was a faint glimmer underneath her eyelids. She said telepathically, *Steve. He hurt Dendera.*

"Never mind that now," he said hoarsely.

Derrick raced in, took in the scene and dropped to his knees on the other side of Olivia. "Hi, Olivia," the Elf said, his voice strong and calm. "You're going to be all right. Do you hear me? Everything is going to be all right."

Sebastian had seen Derrick reassure injured people a thousand times, on any number of expeditions. It wasn't always the truth. Many had died, comforted by the healer's calm confidence.

Bailey strode back into the workroom just as Tony appeared in the doorway. Bailey's expression had turned harsh and dangerous. She said, "Dendera's dead. She was stabbed in the throat."

Sebastian snapped. "Find Steve. Don't kill him."

"Right," said Tony. He and Bailey disappeared again.

Derrick nudged Sebastian's hands out of the way, scanned Olivia's wound and began to cast a series of spells. "Hang in there, honey," the Elf said. "We've got you now."

The healer sounded so sane.

Sebastian wasn't, not in the slightest. He went to a place far beyond sanity or pride. He lay down on the floor beside Olivia and put his lips to her ear. "Olivia, please don't leave me," he whispered. "I'm begging you."

He was right. Her eyes weren't quite shut.

She blinked and said, *I won't.*

Just then, Derrick also spoke in his head. *Sebastian.*

He snapped his head up and stared at the other male, his entire body breaking into a cold sweat.

The Elf smiled at him and nodded. Derrick wasn't lying to reassure a dying woman.

She really was going to be okay.

Sebastian grew dizzy, the relief was so intense. He pressed his lips to the tender skin at her temple. "I don't need your permission," he said to her. "I'm going to start looking out for you now."

She turned her head slightly, into his caress. *That's fine by me.*

Derrick leaned forward. "Olivia, don't be alarmed. I want to put you to sleep now so I can work on you without worrying that I might cause you any pain. I promise that you're going to wake up in a few hours feeling much better. Is that all right with you?"

"Yes?" she whispered uncertainly. She opened her eyes, and her gaze cut sideways to Sebastian.

He brushed his lips against hers. "I've trusted Derrick with my life more times than I can count. Go to sleep and I will see you in a few hours."

Derrick cast the spell and she was out before he finished speaking.

Tony and Bailey reappeared in the open doorway. They looked furious and worried at the same time. Bailey's gaze went immediately to Olivia. "How is she?"

"I have work to do," said Derrick. "She needs a transfusion of blood, and all I have is saline solution. The knife also struck much too close to her pulmonary artery for my liking." The Elf sat back on his heels and looked around at the trio of worried faces. "Is this one of those times when I'm telling you too much information?"

"Yes," Sebastian and Bailey said at the same time.

Sebastian asked, "Where's Steve?"

"He's gone," Bailey said. "Well, I can't be absolutely sure about that, because we didn't search every single inch of the island. But all the evidence says he's left. A wetsuit is missing from the washroom, and all the rest have been slashed, so we checked the tanks on the beach. There's one tank missing, and he let the oxygen out from all the rest. He must have been planning this for a while." She scowled down at Olivia as Derrick worked on her. "We had to have just missed him. We watched for threats from everywhere else, but we didn't watch each other. Most of us can't make the crossover without suits and tanks."

Sebastian stood. Bailey was right. She was Light Fae, Derrick was an Elf and Tony and Olivia were human. None of them could hold their breath and swim in the frigid water for the ten minutes or so that it would take to reach the other side.

Like everyone else, Sebastian had used a suit and a tank to cross over, but that was more for comfort, not survival. As a Wyr, he generated more body heat than any of the others, and he had a powerful set of lungs.

Rage settled in him as an unshakable purpose. "You might not be able to make the crossover, but I can."

"Make him hurt," said Bailey. "Make him hurt real bad."

"Count on it," Sebastian told her.

He paused to look down at Olivia, his heart squeezing tight. He said to his people, "She's going to be my mate."

They all exchanged looks. None of them appeared surprised, but then they had all watched Sebastian with Olivia over the last week.

Derrick told him, "Trust me. Trust her."

"I do," he said.

He strode out of the cottage, shapeshifted and took wing to fly over the water. Then he shifted again in midair, rolled and dived toward the passageway. Lunging through the water as fast as he could, he thought ahead to what he would find.

Phaedra would be on watch, but the Djinn would only be on the lookout for people trying to approach the crossover passageway from Earth. She was expecting for the team to emerge from the Other land. She wouldn't know to stop Steve.

Had Steve still been close enough to feel Olivia's cry for help?

While the question renewed his rage, it was probably irrelevant. One way or another, as soon as Steve had made his move, he would have known that he would have to work fast. He couldn't know whether or not Phaedra would say anything to the crew circling in the yacht at the surface. He would be swimming as fast as he could underwater, to get as much distance from the yacht as he could before surfacing, which was why he needed an oxygen tank even though he was also Wyr.

Steve had to have a preplanned route in mind. Perhaps he was meeting someone, but if he was, Sebastian doubted very much if they would chance connecting too close to Phaedra or the yacht. Just like with the crossover passageway, it would be much easier for someone to slip away than for someone to try to approach.

Then Sebastian knew where Steve was going.

The other Wyr was going to try for one of the underwater openings to an old, vast tunnel system that lay underneath San Francisco. Carling had told him about it. When Vampyres traveled back and forth from the island, they would swim to the tunnel system to avoid surfacing in any sunlight. If Steve reached the tunnels, his chances for disappearing grew a lot higher. He might even be planning to meet someone in the city.

Sebastian swam harder, pushing his body to the limit. His lungs began to burn. He needed to breathe.

He reached the other side of the passageway and sensed Phaedra's presence.

She sensed him too. She said, sounding sleepy and bored, *It's about time you all started to come out.*

We're not, he said as he kicked upward. *Steve killed Dendera, stabbed Olivia and sabotaged our equipment.*

He broke the water's surface and sucked air.

Phaedra's physical form snapped into existence in front of him. She looked strange, as she didn't swim, but merely appeared as if she stood in front of him on dry land.

"He stabbed Olivia?"

"Yes."

The Djinn scowled. "I'm very displeased. Grace will be unhappy. That will make my father furious."

"She's going be all right." He cocked his head, treading water. "Are you bored enough to track Steve down? I think he's headed for some tunnels underneath the city."

"I will do much better than that." She vanished, then reappeared again almost instantly with Steve wrapped in her arms, complete with wetsuit, flippers, mask, oxygen tank and the container of books hanging from him by a cord. "You were correct," she said. "He was just beginning to crawl into a tunnel when I found him."

Steve kicked and struggled, wriggling like a fish on the end of a line. Behind the mask, Sebastian caught a glimpse of the other man's astonished expression.

It swiftly turned to fear as Sebastian lunged for his throat.

Sebastian didn't kill the other man, but he did hurt him real bad. He had told Bailey he would, and he always kept his word.

Steve tried to fight, but he didn't have a chance. Sebastian was, by far, the better and more seasoned fighter. In fact there was no comparison. Steve was hampered with the weight of the oxygen tank, the heavy container of books, and the mouthpiece and mask that obscured his face when he attempted to shapeshift to bite.

Sebastian drove his fist into that mask. Then he did it again, and again. The blows broke the lens and drove pieces of the frame into the other man's face. They twisted together, bobbing with the waves, while Phaedra floated close by and watched curiously. Sebastian felt other bones break underneath his hands. They sank underneath the water, and he was all right with that. All he could see was the wide pool of blood where Olivia had lain.

Then other people splashed into the water alongside them. They shouted at Sebastian and worked to tear the two men apart. Sebastian recognized members of his crew from the yacht. Only then did he let go of Steve.

The symbologist lolled half-conscious as Sebastian's crew dragged him onto the yacht. A couple of them hauled on the line to draw up the container. Ignoring the chilly air, Sebastian climbed up the ladder, issuing orders like a spray of bullets.

"He murdered Dendera and sabotaged our equipment. I need suits and tanks. Guard the hell out of that container. I think he was working with somebody who wants the contents badly. He had to have expected to disappear fast otherwise he never would have tried to pull this stunt. Call Carling, Julian and the tribunal, and update everybody. Get someone to comb the tunnels underneath San Francisco. Trace every step that fucker made when he went into the city during shore leave. In fact, trace every step that fucker has made in the last three months." He took a deep breath and roared, *"Where's my equipment?"*

They came running with two spare suits and tanks. Then Brendan, who was captain of the yacht in his absence, said, "Just so you know, all the research teams have reported back. Their reports are sitting on your desk."

"What?" Sebastian stared at him, for a moment not connecting at all to what the other man was saying. "Forget about all that."

He hooked his arms through straps on the tanks, grabbed the suits and dove into the water again. He had to get back to the island as fast as he could.

His mate needed him.

Chapter Ten

When Olivia opened her eyes, she lay in her bed in the manor house. Faded sunlight streamed into the window, touching the edges of things inside the room one last time before disappearing for another night. A bright fire crackled in the hearth.

Sebastian slumped in an armchair beside the bed. His head rested against the back of the chair, his eyes closed.

She was quite free from pain, clean and warm, and tucked under blankets. Then she tried to move, and her heart leaped into a rapid, skittish tempo. Her mouth dried out, and her head swam. A saline bag hung from one of the bedposts, the line running to an IV taped to the back of her left hand.

Sebastian's eyes flared open. He straightened and leaned over her.

She had grown used to the strange black-and-amber pattern in his eyes. He looked so tired, worn and worried. "Don't try to move around too much," he said. "You've lost a lot of blood."

"Dendera," she said.

"I'm sorry." He stroked her face.

Moisture flooded her eyes. She nodded and turned her face away.

The chair creaked as he shifted. Then the bed tilted as he sat on the edge. He planted his hands flat on the mattress on either side of her head and leaned closer. "Hey," he said. "Look at me."

As always, he pulled her to him. She could never turn away from him. She looked up. His hard face looked even more haggard at that angle, the fire throwing strong, flickering bands of light and shadow across the room.

He told her softly, "You know we need to talk, don't you?"

Her mouth shook. She didn't trust herself to speak, so she just nodded again. Why would he bring that up now, of all times?

He stroked her hair. "In fact," he said, "I've been planning on talking to you for a while. I was just waiting for the right time. And this is not the right time at all, so naturally I want to take full advantage of that."

She blinked several times. "I don't understand. What do you mean?"

He smiled. There was something remarkably patient, clear-eyed and ruthless about him in that moment. "I love you," he said. "And I believe you love me."

She whispered, "Yes."

Gently, gently he bent down and brushed her lips with his. "Then this is what we're going to do. You're going to marry me. We'll winter in Jamaica and live the rest of the year in Louisville. You will work part-time at your job. I will work part-time running my company, and Bailey will take over the rest. We'll have children—I think two would be nice—and we'll have plenty of time to take care of them. And we'll travel sometimes, but mostly we'll stay at home, and if I go blind, I will find an avian Wyr who will fly with me sometimes—"

"That's not going to happen," she interrupted.

"I understand, but if it does…"

"It *won't*."

He cocked his head and looked exasperated. "I am trying to make a point here."

In spite of everything that had happened and the dizziness that still swam in her mind, she had to smile. "And what point is that?"

"That we can meet every challenge ahead of us if we do it together."

Her smile turned into a chuckle, while happiness began to take root. "Is that what you were saying underneath all of those orders?"

"They were statements of fact, not orders," he said. He touched her cheek lightly with the backs of his fingers. "And we're not really having that talk, not while you're injured and exhausted. That would be insensitive of me. Besides, it's too soon. I'm merely making things easy for you by laying everything out ahead of time."

Her chuckle turned into a helpless ghost of a laugh. "All of that was preparation for the talk we're going to have someday?"

"Exactly."

"Well, that's good to know, because it *is* too soon for all of it," she whispered. "I can look forward to the fact that when we do have that talk at the appropriate time, you will actually propose with a question and a ring, and not a statement of fact."

His expression went blank. "A ring."

It occurred to Olivia that she had recently grown to care about more than one creature that wasn't housebroken. That was when her meager strength petered out. She closed her eyes. "Goodnight, Sebastian."

"Sleep well, my love."

He kissed her forehead, and that was the last thing she remembered for a long time.

Of course, things were not as simple and as straightforward as the talk they planned on having one day. She slept, woke and drank some warm broth, and slept some more. Sebastian was always present when she opened her eyes. Derrick checked on her a few times through the day, and by the next evening he had removed the IV.

She had to work through the memory of the attack, and the shock of witnessing Dendera's murder. Sebastian was there for that too. He held her as she wiped her eyes and talked through the worst of it.

Olivia could not make the underwater crossing until she had recovered from the chest injury and could complete a few basic exercises, like walk a mile in under twelve minutes. She was healthy, though, not only in body but in spirit, and she rebounded quickly.

Soon she could sit in the main hall in the evenings and visit with Derrick, Tony and Bailey. Then she could take short walks. She shooed Sebastian back to work, while she sat in the sun and read the light novels they brought to her.

In the meantime, the other four worked hard. They transported the part of the collection that Olivia, Dendera and Steve had already packed. Time passed more quickly on Earth, so every time they made the crossing there was more news.

Steve had been taken into official custody. Through emails, phone calls and bank account records, investigators discovered that, after Carling had completed background checks and hired everybody, a private collector from South America had approached him with a two-million-dollar bribe and a wish list of items. Shortly after that, the collector was taken into custody and extradited to the Elder tribunal in the States for prosecution.

With the approval of the tribunal, Carling hired a new team of symbologists to finish packing the library. "You are also certainly welcome to stay and finish working on the job if you so choose," Carling wrote in a letter to Olivia, which Bailey delivered one afternoon. "But even if you do, you will need help, and besides, I want for you to have the freedom to come home if you should wish."

Olivia was tempted briefly, mostly because she refused to let another person's actions drive her away from what she loved to do. But, the truth be told, she had grown a little weary of the adventure.

What finalized her decision, however, was when Bailey handed Sebastian a sealed packet in silence. He tore the packet open and looked through the contents quickly. Afterward, he set the papers on the kitchen table and walked out of the house, into the overgrown vegetable garden.

Bailey and Olivia looked at each other soberly. Then Olivia picked up the first report and scanned it. "Sorry to say, this approach to breaking the curse is not a feasible one…"

She set it aside and picked up the next one. "I'm afraid we found no realistic avenue in the indigenous magic system that would alleviate what has been done…"

And a third. "I cannot express in words how difficult it is to tell you that we found nothing…"

She stopped reading, pushed away from the table and walked outside to look for Sebastian. She found him standing at the edge of the cliff, his hands on his hips as he stared out over the water. He looked severe, unapproachable, his back stiff and his face like stone, but she didn't let any of that stop her.

She walked up beside him and slipped an arm around his waist. "Of course this is not the appropriate time to have that talk that we've been planning, so let me tell you how things are going to be," she said gently. "Then we will talk about it when the time is right. You will propose to me with a beautiful diamond ring, because I have my heart set on it. When we get married, I will wear the dress of my dreams, because I have my heart set on that as well. You are going to wear a tuxedo-gray morning suit, and Bailey is going to be your best person, so you need to remember to ask her soon. But first, right now, you and I are quitting this job. You are going to delegate the rest of it, and we are going to cross over, go to Florida and consult with Grace. And we are going to start facing our challenges together."

The tension in his body eased somewhat as she spoke. He slipped an arm around her shoulders as he said, "You're not ready to scuba dive."

"I am too," she told him. "I can walk a mile."

He shook his head. "I don't believe you're under twelve minutes yet."

"It doesn't matter. I'm close enough." When he opened his mouth to argue, she covered his lips with one hand. "It's a brief trip. Derrick will come with us, and he'll monitor me the whole time. Sebastian, it's time to go."

He looked at her with so much pain in his cursed eyes.

It broke her heart. She loved him so very much.

So they would come full circle, back to Florida. It was not quite where everything had begun, but it was where the most important thing had begun—it was where they had first met.

Sebastian refused to let her swim at all during the crossover, and when she protested, Derrick backed him up until she threw up her hands and let them have their way. While she forced herself to remain passive, Sebastian held her in his arms and did all the work.

In the end she was grateful for it. Breathing from the oxygen tank seemed to take much more effort than it had the first time. Her chest ached, and the dry air irritated her lungs.

On the other side of the crossing, she sensed Phaedra's presence a split second before the Djinn surrounded her and the world fell away. When reality solidified again, she and Phaedra were standing on the deck of the yacht. While water streamed off Olivia's wetsuit, Phaedra looked perfectly dry.

One of the crew members shouted a greeting from the pilot's cabin. She waved at them. Then she removed her mouthpiece, pushed back her mask and took a deep breath of fresh air as she looked around her. Sebastian was nowhere to be seen.

Angling out her jaw, she said, "You forgot Sebastian, dimwit."

Phaedra shrugged, her eyes narrowed. "I didn't forget him. He knows how to swim."

She sighed. "In any case, you've got to stop transporting people without their permission."

"I don't see why," said Phaedra as she crossed her arms. "Sometimes it can be quite useful."

Olivia pinched her nose. Now she knew from personal experience why Grace had said, *Oh I don't know why I bother.*

Phaedra studied her. The Djinn's expression turned serious. "You are better now? The damage has repaired itself?"

"More or less," she said. She shrugged out of the heavy oxygen tank and left it on the deck as she walked to the railing to watch for Sebastian.

Phaedra walked to her side and touched her shoulder. As Olivia looked at her, Phaedra said simply, "I'm glad."

Surprise softened her irritation. She reached up to touch Phaedra's hand. The Djinn did not pull away from her overture. Wow, she thought. It made Phaedra seem almost warm and cuddly.

They both watched as Sebastian exploded to the water's surface. He sliced through the water and climbed up the hull ladder. Olivia looked from his furious expression to Phaedra's impervious one. She decided she did not need to be a part of their upcoming conversation, so she left to shower and change into street clothes.

Sebastian had been tempted to ask Phaedra for a ride to Florida, but after her latest stunt, he refused to even consider it. Instead, he chartered a plane and they spent the flight mostly in silence. He bought a pile of newspapers and magazines, and they passed the time looking through everything. Three months had passed on Earth.

At one point, Olivia said, "This is the strangest, worst case of jet lag I've ever experienced, and that's not even taking into account traveling from coast to coast."

"It can take a couple of weeks to re-acclimate," he said, his voice toneless. The ground glass was back in his chest, and even that much conversation was an effort.

He thought she understood, because she took one of his hands between hers and didn't say anything more.

Once they landed in Miami, they took a car service to Grace and Khalil's house.

Olivia had called ahead, so they knew that Grace and Khalil waited at home for their arrival. Sebastian's heart began to pound as the car pulled up to the front of an attractive ranch house. They climbed out. He reached for Olivia's hand as they walked up the path, and she squeezed his fingers.

When he rang the doorbell, a pretty, titian-haired young woman answered the door. She rushed forward and threw her arms around Olivia, and the two women murmured to each other as they hugged.

A massive male Djinn walked up beside them. Khalil had white, regal features, long raven hair held back with a strip of leather and those typical, piercing, diamond-like eyes. Phaedra looked a lot like her father.

"Come in," Grace said. She kept an arm around Olivia's waist as she said, "I asked Atefeh and Ebrahim to babysit Max and Chloe so we could have time to ourselves without the children. I have been so worried about you. Are you really better?"

"Almost a hundred percent," said Olivia with a small smile.

The ground glass in Sebastian's chest shifted, cutting at him. His voice was harsh as he said, "You know why we're here. I need to petition you."

Khalil frowned, but Grace turned to Sebastian immediately. Even though her face was young, her hazel gaze was filled with a kind of compassion that seemed ageless. "Please, come sit and talk with me," she said.

Somehow there was an indefinable yet essential shift in Power, and it was the Oracle that spoke to him.

Sebastian followed her to a gleaming oak dinner table with six matching chairs, set in front of ceiling high windows that looked over the ocean. The Oracle sat at one end of the table, and gestured for Sebastian to sit at her right. He complied, while Olivia and Khalil remained several steps away, present but not participating.

The Oracle said, "Tell me your story."

It poured out of him in a convulsive rush, while she listened in silence. Finally he stopped speaking and watched her.

The Oracle frowned, her gaze unfocused, and rubbed the polished surface of the table with her fingertips. Then her lips moved silently. She looked for all the world as if she were talking to herself.

Sebastian clenched his hands into fists.

He thought, This is where she tells me there is no hope. This is the final answer to my question.

Suddenly he couldn't bear to wear his sunglasses for one more moment. He tore them off and flung them across the room. They shattered to pieces against the opposite wall.

The peripheral vision on his right side was almost completely gone, but he still sensed the Djinn shifting in unfriendly reaction.

Then the Oracle's expression underwent a drastic change.

"Khalil," she bit out. "Please retrieve that shrunken head from Jamaica for me, will you?"

"As you wish," said the Djinn. His physical form dissipated, and he blew away.

Sebastian and Olivia had no time to do anything other than exchange one mystified look. Then Khalil returned again to place the shrunken head in the Oracle's hands, his expression filled with distaste.

The Oracle spoke again, silently. This time she appeared to be arguing. Her expression flashed with anger. She slapped a flattened hand on the table and barked out, "You will obey!"

Her Power shifted. To Sebastian's magical sense, she seemed to reach out, grasp hold of an insubstantial something and shake it.

The next voice that poured out of her mouth was not hers. The rapid words it spoke were not English, but an indigenous language that was, to Sebastian, all too familiar.

Before he could react, Power flared out of the shrunken head. It cut through him like a saber and blasted him out of his chair.

Then with a snap, the Power disappeared.

Disoriented, his head ringing, Sebastian struggled to his hands and knees. Dimly he became aware that Olivia had fallen to her knees beside him. She flung her arms around him. "Are you all right?"

"I don't know," he heard himself say.

Nearby, Grace said in horror, "Oh my God, I really am holding a *shrunken head.*"

The Djinn said in a gentle voice, "Yes, Gracie. I will just remove that object from this house forever, shall I?"

"Pleeeeeassse."

Olivia cupped Sebastian's face. Her hands were shaking. "Sebastian, look at me."

He tried to focus on her. Everything in his head throbbed.

"Your eyes," she whispered. "The black—it's all gone."

He shook his head and then wished he hadn't. Carefully he shifted to sit cross-legged on the floor. "Your face is blurry. Everything is blurry."

Grace said, "It will probably take a few weeks for your vision to return to normal."

He blinked in her direction. "What did you do?"

"For the first time in my life," Grace said grimly, "I forced a ghost to do something. And I'm not sorry, either. That chieftain was a snot. Feel free to use the guest room if you need to lie down." A chair scraped across the floor. "Now, if you'll excuse me, I think I'll go wash my hands in Purell for a couple of hours."

The sound of her footsteps retreated.

Holy hell. Did Grace just say what he thought she'd said?

Carling had been right all along. They had needed the chieftain to use the shrunken head to lift the curse. It had been a totally impossible solution that had, somehow, still happened.

"Okay," he said. "Okay."

He groped behind him. The wall was nearby. He shifted over until he could lean his back against it. Only some time afterward did he realize that he had kept such a clenched hold on Olivia, he had forced her to scoot over with him. He pulled her onto his lap, bowing around her as she wrapped her arms around his neck.

After a few minutes, she loosened her hold enough to pull back and study him. He wasn't sure, but he thought she looked shell-shocked, thrilled and concerned.

"Come on," she said. "Let's go to the guest room."

He let her pull him to his feet. Taking his hand, she led him down the hallway. Wary of his blurred vision, he walked carefully, reaching out once to touch the hallway wall.

They walked into a quiet, shadowed bedroom where he eased himself down on a large bed. He stretched out with a sigh. That cutting blast of Power had been just like the first time. His body was still reacting to the adrenaline dump. All of his muscles shook with a fine tremor.

She stroked his hair. "Sebastian?"

"I'm all right," he said. "Just, holy fuck."

"That scared me half to death." Her voice wobbled. "Did it hurt?"

"It happened too fast to hurt, but I have a headache now."

"Let me get you some medicine," she said. "Then you can rest for as long as you need."

"Only if you lie down with me," he told her.

"Of course." She walked away, and a few moments later she returned with a glass of water and aspirin. He gulped both of them down, groped to put the empty glass on the nightstand and then stretched out again while she pulled off his shoes, then lay beside him.

He pulled her into his arms. Holding her felt incredible. Her body's soft, warm weight was the essential something that he had needed for a long time, and in a few short weeks she had become his bedrock.

He pressed his lips against her forehead and murmured, "We both got a little beat up recently, didn't we?"

A snort escaped her. "A little. But it's all over now, thank God. Just rest."

And so he did, turning his face into her hair and eventually drifting into a light doze. When he stirred, his headache had eased and the bedroom had grown darker.

He tensed and gripped her shoulder. "Tell me the bedroom really is darker."

Olivia sat up. She said in a strong voice, "Yes, it really is darker. It's evening now. Here, let me get the light."

He put his hands at her waist, bracing her as she leaned over him to click on the bedside light. Brightness flooded the bedroom, and he squinted as he looked around.

His vision had still not cleared completely, but it wasn't as blurry as it had been earlier. He let his gaze linger over the details in the stylish room before he turned his face up to look at Olivia, who remained draped over him.

Her gorgeous face broke into a smile as she searched his gaze.

"It's gone," she told him. "All of that black is really, really gone. Your eyes are the most beautiful things I've ever seen."

"You are the most beautiful thing I've ever seen." He cupped the back of her head, pulled her down to him and kissed her.

He knew, realistically, that it would take just as long to get used to the absence of the emotional weight from that curse as it would to physically recover, and he looked forward to every delicious minute of it.

She whispered against his lips, "Tell me that again when I know you've fully recovered your eyesight in a couple of weeks."

"I don't need to wait any longer," he said. "I can see quite clearly right now."

He could, too.

They had a wealth of time in front of them, and their future had never seemed brighter or more full of promise than it did in that moment.

He rolled her onto her back and lost himself in kissing her. The way she molded her body to align against him, the way her soft mouth felt against his, her lips, her lips were so goddamned unique.

"You know you're mine, don't you?" he muttered. "You have to be. You just have to be."

"Of course I'm yours," she whispered. She cupped his face in both hands. "Just as you are mine. I may not be Wyr, Sebastian. But you are still my mate."

That was it. That was what he needed to hear from her. She was so wise. Her spirit would always pull at him. He swallowed hard as moisture flooded his eyes.

He pulled at her clothes, working to get her undressed, and she helped him. Then she turned her attention to his, and soon they lay together, skin to skin. Soon after that he eased inside of her, and together they shared the most necessary, most moving of all rhythms.

He cupped her breast, molding it gently as he rocked his hips against the sweet curve of her pelvis. Watching her open, tender expression as she peaked in climax was the highest privilege he had ever been granted. He lost all sense of control, all sense of a separate self, as he spilled his own climax into her welcoming body.

Yes, he took her. But he gave himself to her as well. He gave her everything he had.

And now it was time that he and Olivia started having that talk.

About the Author

Thea Harrison resides in Colorado. She wrote her first book, a romance, when she was nineteen and had sixteen romances published under the name Amanda Carpenter.

She took a break from writing to collect a couple of graduate degrees and a grown child. Her graduate degrees are in Philanthropic Studies and Library Information Science, but her first love has always been writing fiction. She's back with her paranormal Elder Races series. You can check out her website at: www.theaharrison.com, and also follow her on Twitter http://twitter.com/TheaHarrison and on Facebook at www.facebook.com/TheaHarrison.

Look for these titles from Thea Harrison

THE ELDER RACES SERIES

Published by Berkley

Dragon Bound

Half-human and half-wyr, Pia Giovanni spent her life keeping a low profile among the wyrkind and avoiding the continuing conflict between them and their Dark Fae enemies. But after being blackmailed into stealing a coin from the hoard of a dragon, Pia finds herself targeted by one of the most powerful–and passionate—of the Elder Races.

As the most feared and respected of the wyrkind, Dragos Cuelebre cannot believe someone had the audacity to steal from him, much less succeed. And when he catches the thief, Dragos spares her life, claiming her as his own to further explore the desire they've ignited in one another.

Storm's Heart
Serpent's Kiss
Oracle's Moon
Lord's Fall
Kinked

ELDER RACES NOVELLAS

Published by Samhain Publishing

True Colors
Natural Evil
Devil's Gate
Hunter's Season

AMANDA CARPENTER ROMANCES

Published by Samhain Publishing

A Deeper Dimension

The Wall

A Damaged Trust

The Great Escape

Flashback

OTHER WORKS BY THEA HARRISON

Dragos Takes a Holiday
Divine Tarot (Print Ed. True Colors & Natural Evil)
Destiny's Tarot (Print Ed. Devil's Gate & Hunter's Season)

Printed in Great Britain
by Amazon